C000121128

THE NOELLE SITUATION

Iona Stuart

Happy Birthday, Keren!
Enjoy!

Iona Stuart

The Noelle Situation

Copyright © 2020 Iona Stuart

All rights reserved.

The characters and events portrayed in this book are fictitious. Any similarities to real persons, living or dead, is coincidental and not intended by the author.

No part of this book may be reproduced, or stored in a retrieval system, or transmitted in any form or by any means, electronic, mechanical, photocopying, recording, or otherwise, without express written permission of the publisher.

The author may be contacted at: ionamstuart@gmail.com

ISBN: 979-8-6706-7135-4

CONTENTS

CHAPTER 1

It was Friday, September 6th, at 15:00 when Phoenix Hudson found herself sitting in a therapist's office.

The chair was solid beneath her, her own body feeling unnaturally heavy where she sat. It was as if her whole being were melting into the fabric, sinking into the floor, melding into the very structure of the building. She could hear the rhythmic ticking of a clock somewhere behind her head—out of sight, but far from out of mind—and the way its penetrating sound syncopated with her heartbeat, creating some sort of sardonic melody. The walls were painted in passive pastel colors, supposedly to soothe those who found themselves trapped within them. The floor was a dotted linoleum, scuffed with a thousand frustrated footprints. The door creaked behind her as the therapist entered.

Phoenix watched as the woman took a seat opposite her, crossing her legs, placing her arms casually upon her knees. She pushed her glasses from the base of her nose up to rest at the bridge and smiled. Never in her life had Phoenix seen a smile like that which she had trusted. There was something in smiles like that, a sort of patronizing pity, which made her feel ill at ease. She studied the woman's face carefully, from the light gloss on her lips, to the faint crow's feet beginning to appear at the corner of her eyes.

"So," the woman began, "how are things?"

Phoenix shrugged. She didn't know what to say.

"You don't know?"

"No," Phoenix sighed, and ran a hand through her dark brown locks as they fell over her shoulders.

"You don't know, or you don't want to say?"

Phoenix shrugged again. She could see the therapist's eyes wandering over her from behind their glass shields, absorbing all the images and information that painted her external being, trying to work their way through the façade and into the twisting pathways of her brain.

Phoenix took a deep and shaky breath. "Maybe the best thing I can say is that I think too much."

"In what way?"

She let out a long sigh and readjusted herself in the seat. "Do you ever stop and wonder how things got to where they are?"

"What do you mean?"

"How something that once was Not became something that Is?"

The therapist nodded. "Tell me more about what you mean."

"You see, there are things I have learned over the years, be them few, and I'm more aware than you know of what life Is and Is Not. Of what is Acceptable and Acceptable Not. Of what is Said and what is Said Not…

"It's like sometimes I open my eyes and I find myself somewhere completely alien, in a life that doesn't even feel like my own."

"Well," the woman's eyebrows furrowed lightly, in that look of sympathy that psych workers use to try and make their patients feel understood, "you've experienced a lot of change in the last year."

Phoenix barely registered the woman's responses; she was simply staring ahead of herself in a daze.

"Monachopsis," she said, at last, the word leaving her mouth in a strange stream of sound that didn't feel like her own.

The therapist looked at her quizzically. "What?"

"Monachopsis—*the subtle but persistent feeling of being out of place, unable to recognize the ambient roar of your intended habitat, in which you'd be fluidly, brilliantly, effortlessly at home.*"

"Is that how you feel?"

"I don't know what I feel, all I know is that I don't understand anything anymore. It just all seems wrong."

"Is this about Noelle?" the therapist inquired.

There was a momentary pause, a slight hesitation, a deep-rooted feeling that rose in the young girl that made her wary of discussing so much so soon—and doing so to a complete stranger.

Then Phoenix nodded, "Yes."

"And how did she make you feel?"

"I loved her."

"At the beginning, or the end?"

"Both," Phoenix replied plainly, her eyes staring straight ahead of her, staring at the same spot on the floor, unfaltering, "a part of me doesn't think I'll ever stop."

"And did you always feel like that?"

Phoenix nodded. "I'd like very much to say that, in the beginning, everything was great. But nothing is ever great. And all my regret signifies that I am always reckless, and this was no exception."

"And why do you say that?"

"Because there were times, on multiple occasions, when the world just seemed to stop spinning, and she was the only one who filled my mind. And that's just ridiculous. Look where that got me. It was all careless, all reckless, and now here I am. Because it was all in my mind."

The woman shifted subtly in her seat, nodding slowly at the words Phoenix had to say—nodding in that way they did. It was all just *that way they did*; nothing personal, just business.

"Because you loved her?"

Phoenix sighed a deep, disconsolate sigh.

"When you think about the idea of love, it seems so simple. It's something that follows you your entire life: in games that you play in your childhood; in conversations with friends during teen sleepovers; in chick flicks and magazines; in the warm smells of summer sweetness and winter cinnamon; in the songs of birds and lyrical words of the wise. But it isn't the same when it happens to you; it wasn't the same when it happened to me—when it happened to Juniper.

"When it happens to you, the smiling, happy, perfectly contented image is a very small fraction of it. Love is hard to live with, and impossible to live without. When it happens to you, love is pain, love is suffering, love is compromise, and love is complicated. Hell, there is nothing at all about this whole situation that isn't complicated. And I've somehow managed to land myself in the middle of it all."

"That's how you feel?" The therapist flickered her gaze between the girl sitting opposite her and the pen poised above the pad of paper she used to record her patients' deepest and darkest of secrets. "As if you've landed in the middle of it all? Of all these complications?"

Phoenix nodded, "And it was all of my own doing. Thus, proving my recklessness."

"Why do you believe it was your own doing? What makes you feel like this was your fault?"

"I made connections that were never meant to be connected," Phoenix felt her nose tingle as tears threatened to push their way into her eyes, but she fought them down, taking a slight gulp.

"I put together jigsaw pieces that fit so perfectly but were never supposed to be together. To think that the love you feel is just some wandering thought in the back of your head is a difficult process to comprehend. The seemingly eternal hours spent in sheer contemplation, just envisaging every possible outcome under the sun, those are the hardest. On one shoulder to be told that somehow, somewhere, just maybe it will all work out; on the other, to be perfectly informed that you can warrant it no better. And the vibrant colors all around you can suddenly fade to gray."

The woman nodded, soaking in all the information, filing the words into her brain, to later scribble down and file literally into the sleek cabinet to her right. Phoenix could see it in the way she moved her head, in the way her eyes studied her as she sat—it was as if she could see the cogs whirring in her mind, working to produce the right response, the correct line of questioning.

"So, you feel as if the light has been taken out of you? Almost as if everything that was bright has been moved into a shadowy and gray part of yourself. That seems a bit self-deprecating, don't you think? Almost as if you blame yourself for what took place, perhaps? Why is that?"

"It's such a fine line, you see," Phoenix replied slowly, her eyes wandering over the dots on the floor, creating constellations in her mind, "the one between eternal happiness and everlasting sorrow; the line between wondrous dreams and harsh reality. Everyone must be thrust back into the waking world at the end of the night, but whether it's to watch the beauty of the morning sun or see the only light in your life to be crudely blown out is what's important. It's the steps you take, the actions required, and the consequences of these actions. It will either make you stronger or break you into nothing."

She looked up at the therapist, making direct eye contact for the first time during their session. "And I'm afraid for me it's done the latter."

The therapist sat back in her seat and sighed, rubbing her chin lightly with a slender forefinger. She placed her hand back on her pad and let her left arm relax over the chair slightly; static, hovering, resting with reflection.

"I think, again, that it's the self-deprecating side of you that feels that way. As if this part of Phoenix won't let the other atone for the events that have preceded all that's taken place. Won't let her say, 'Wait a minute, this wasn't my fault, I wasn't the only person involved here.' Don't you think?"

Phoenix simply shrugged.

"Fine," the therapist nodded once more, "why don't you tell me how it all began, then?"

Phoenix took a deep and shaky breath. She wasn't sure she wanted to do that. She wasn't sure she knew *how* to do that. But if she couldn't say it now, here, to this person, then how would she ever say it at all? How would she ever be able to try and make sense of this mess that had become her life? This mess she had made. This mess in which she was now stuck. "All of this started with a nightmare. No, wait... That's not right. All of this started with a classroom."

•••

It had been a somewhat gray day toward the end of the month of August when Phoenix had found herself once more thrown into the routine of work.

To say it had been specifically taxing would have been a lie; perhaps it had been a little more difficult to adjust to the early morning rises and the long days—especially compared to the lazy days of summer, to which she had become so accustomed in the previous few weeks—but it was never *truly* difficult. And although it was work, it was of the kind that everyone must experience in some manner in their lives—one that holds different meaning and thought to all. This being, of course, high school.

For Phoenix, high school was a place of escape. Somewhere that she could temporarily put the real world on hold, and just concentrate on what she had in front of her. A (somewhat) clear-cut line between what's expected and what should be done. A simple map of daily routines to be followed. A place where wandering minds were free to explore without commitment. And, most importantly, a place where the decisions made seemed only to impact the immediate world around her and promised not to reach anything greater as time went on.

That's where Phoenix went wrong.

Somehow, somewhere along the line, she'd gotten them mixed up. The world of things that are real, and the world of high school adventures.

The old school building seemed to open up before her all at once when she rounded the corner at the end of the street that morning. Students streamed in from all angles, snaking in and out of the triple-arched porch that stood on pillars before the main doors: the girls smiled and laughed and embraced one another; the boys slapped each other on the back, fist-bumped, and exchanged 'sports hugs.'

The sky above was overcast, causing a shadow to hang over the grounds; the large melancholy eyes of glass that lined the redbrick masonry walls looked as if they had been weeping with the remnants of the previous evening's unexpectant summer rain. Phoenix gazed at the school, feeling like a million years had passed since she had last laid her hazel irises upon its solid frame. She wasn't sure what to make of that feeling. She wasn't happy, but neither was she sad. She was simply indifferent to the world around her, as she had learned to be for many years. She took a step toward the main doors, and so the day began.

"Hey!" The voice entered her head as she stood at her locker and caused Phoenix to start. A mere moment later she saw the familiar face appear in front of her as she turned, and she exhaled. "How now, jumpy?"

Phoenix smiled at the blue-haired beauty standing beside her, her cheekbones highlighted by the bulbs that lined the corridor, her chin sharp beneath the silver stud that appeared below her bottom lip, her sapphire eyes blazing in the morning gloom.

"Morning, Juniper. How was your summer?"

Juniper shrugged. "Same old, same old. You?"

"I don't know. The same, I suppose."

Juniper raised a dark eyebrow, the little black hairs that reflected her natural coloring offset by the twinkling silver of the double piercing that sat along its edge.

"You suppose? What does that mean?"

Phoenix sighed. "I just feel like… I don't know. I'm glad to be back." She shook her head lightly. "It's stupid."

"Hey, I'll be the judge of that," Juniper replied. "Tell me, what makes you happy to get back to this hell hole?"

"I…" She thought for a minute. "A part of me just feels like I need to be here, you know? Like, somehow, over the summer, I've missed something. Something important. And that somehow… somehow being back here is going to resolve everything. Replace whatever has been missed."

"Well," Juniper began, "I can't say I understand, but it's not stupid. I mean, we all got our shit, right? And it's okay to feel weird about stuff sometimes and not know why." She wrapped a sylph-like arm around her friend, placing a skeletal ivory hand upon her shoulder, and pulled her into a hug. And Phoenix let her mind stop dwelling on the un-dwellable, grateful for this enduring friendship. "Oh, hey, who do you have for Math this year? Since you were a loser and dropped Art, I'm pretty sure this is the only class we still take together."

"Uh," Phoenix swung her backpack around from her shoulder and ruffled through her bag for her timetable. "Miss Brooks. You?"

Juniper groaned. "Aw, I have Mrs. Pierce."

"Bummer."

"I know! We've always shared a class! I still don't understand why you picked History with Mr. Cold over Art with me. I'd really, *really* hoped we'd be in the same Math class," she sighed. "But you know what they say about hope." Phoenix looked at her quizzically. "It doesn't change anything; it just painfully strings out the inevitable." Phoenix rolled her eyes. "How wonderfully morbid of you, my dear."

Juniper flashed her a cheeky wink. "Aren't I always?"

The bell rang to signify the start of classes, and the school year began anew. Phoenix and Juniper each headed their separate ways as the hallway began to fill with a hundred people bustling to get wherever they were meant to be. Phoenix watched as Juniper walked away, her long blue locks swinging behind her slight frame as she went, before she, too, disappeared into the sea of students.

It was then that Phoenix realized how small she was, and not for the first time. It always astounded her just how many people moved past her in that pre-class rush, and how easily she could just slip to nothing. To become a single grain of sand at the bottom of the Atlantic; a single beam of resonating light from a long-dead star.

Phoenix loved it. It made her feel as if she could be invisible for a second and escape the world. As if she could just fly away, to a far land. A land where she could do *anything*, be *anyone*. It made her feel infinite.

But then the moment passed, and she was standing alone once again in a regular world.

Phoenix arrived at class in what seemed like no time at all that morning. It would seem that she had spent the morning sailing through the seas in her head, and the rest of the world just seemed to escape her, reality fleeting. She pushed her open palm against the wooden door; it was one of the older doors in the building, a hefty mass of peeling wood, held closed by the large hinge situated at the top. It opened with the little amount of strength she gave and led the way into her new Math class for the first time that year.

The walls around her were a dull shade of green, a sort of dusty pine, bordered by a white gloss skirting board—which, by the look of it, had been freshly painted over the summer. The ceiling above her was somewhat faded compared to the bright boards; it was, instead, changing with time from its once supposedly white nature to a cream-ish glow. Three rows of long rectangular lights were fixed into the creamy cloud of a ceiling, and shone down upon the room, glowing faintly in the late morning gloom.

Phoenix liked it. She didn't care that it wasn't as new as the other rooms. Nor did she mind the visible dust floating through the small beams of light escaping from the cloudy overcast on the other side of the windows—something that had, in fact, been a complaint by one of the parents in a previous year on account of their child's asthma. And the cream-colored ceiling did no more than remind her of clouds of dreams. That was something to which she had become accustomed—living in a land of dreams, where all seemed perfect, warm, and safe. It was a place of sanctuary where she could be who she really was, and out in the real world, school was the closest thing to it.

The room had character, and Phoenix liked character. People began to walk past her, joining the ever-growing group of others that were taking their seats around about her. She was snapped back to the world once more; yet for her, it was not quite the real world, not quite as vivid. But simply a classroom, a lesson, a place where things still seemed to hold some degree of sense, and yet to be of little consequence.

Her eyes wandered over the people as they sat, and Phoenix realized that she didn't know where she should go. Though, to say it was a specific quandary would be incorrect. It wasn't a thought at all, really. It wasn't even really a Decision; it was a Not Decision. Just an action that was required to be done.

After a small while of briefly searching her surroundings, she came across the view of two empty seats right at the front of the classroom. And her Not Decision Not Decided that she should probably just sit there.

Yet, perhaps this choice did have an impact on what was to come. Perhaps Phoenix's positioning allowed her meditative state to continue undisturbed. It left her alone at the front; too close to be seen, hiding beneath the piles of papers that overflowed from the desk ahead of her. It was as if she was a shadow sitting on a wall.

So, she took her place and began to remove things from her bag. It was as she was putting her pencil case atop her notebook that she heard the creak of the door as it opened, and as Phoenix looked up at the sound, she walked in.

It was that simple. She walked in. And the world shifted.

CHAPTER 2

*S*eptember 8th

The thing about love that you have to remember is that it's not something that you choose; it's something that chooses you. There are many times in life where love seems like the be-all and end-all of what it takes to be happy, and there are times when love is the reason your chest is weighed down with an anchor so heavy it causes a pain so great that you can feel it in your bones. And the worst part about that? You never know which path it's going to take—and, occasionally, it takes both.

Now, I would love to be one of the blessed few with the talents of illustrating the complexities that life has to offer in words so wonderful and grotesque that their sickly sweetness causes your heart to burst and your head to spin. But, unfortunately, I am not. Nope. Not even a little bit. This is unfortunate, indeed, because I feel that this may hinder slightly my ability to try and make the world understand what it is that happened... Then again, how can I possibly attempt to describe something that I, myself, am not entirely sure I can fully comprehend? And, let's be honest, who's ever going to read this diary, anyway? I guess, maybe, I'm not trying to make the world understand. I guess, maybe, I'm just trying to make myself understand.

You see, to me the universe can be perceived as a series of numbers; numbers of atoms and compounds; equations of gravity and rotation; measurements of proxemics and spacing. The relationships between an infinite quantity of beautiful equations are what keep my life in line, what keep my world following along the tracks of sense. Without these guidelines, I'm afraid I lose my way.

And that's my problem with love; there is no equation. There is no simple numerical process to calculate and understand this strange partnership between heart and brain that equates to something so powerful that it can change your entire life forever. There are no right and wrong answers, only a lot of gray space.

Gray space. The words echoed around Noelle's head as she stared at the lines on the page in front of her. What was she doing? She was rather sure she hadn't kept a journal since she was about eighteen, so what was she doing here, now, twenty years later, looking down at her very own handwriting on the paper of the notebook she'd picked up from Staples a few days previous.

It was all just an exercise—that's what they called it, right? A way for her to work through her emotions. To try to make sense of all the things that were swirling around inside her brain. But that was the thing: Noelle Davis wasn't really interested in making sense of what was going on in her own brain. It was Phoenix she was thinking about.

How she wished she could tell what was going on in that whirring, complex mind of hers. Was she waiting for her, perhaps? Waiting for the initiation of some conversation to give her some glint of… of what? Happiness? Hope? Closure? Noelle didn't know anymore. With a sigh, she picked up the pen once more.

Without the comfort of my numbers to guide me into the actions of what it is, exactly, that I'm supposed to be doing, I only fear that I've made a mistake somewhere along the line; as if I'm trying to look back and find where I might have gone wrong but somehow all my workings have been erased. And in times like this I find there is only one thing I can do, only one thing I know that will clarify my findings; I just have to start again from the beginning, and go through the process of working it all out…

Perhaps that was why she was writing the diary.

•••

The long weeks of the previous year's summer sun had passed by faster than Noelle could keep track, and before she knew it, August was upon her once again. It was always a balancing act, she found, at that time of year; one half of her hated the idea of work and early mornings, the other yearned for nothing more than to be useful and needed again. It was a strange world, the one in which she made her work, filled with those peculiar creatures that are somewhere between functioning adults and bumbling infants—most commonly referred to as *teenagers*.

Noelle hadn't always wanted to be a teacher. In fact, it hadn't even crossed her mind until her mid-twenties, when she suddenly found herself fresh out of university with a degree in mathematics, four years' worth of student debt, and no job prospects in sight. It was her mother who first suggested she go into teaching in that 'just some food for thought' way of hers that, despite her protests, were anything but *just* light food for thought.

And suddenly she'd found her days filled to the brim with creating lesson plans, replacing the batteries of forty-two department calculators, ordering textbooks, and separating lined from graph paper. How riveting. Her friends—non-teacher friends, that is— never understood this decision, never understood why she'd want to spend her days trying her hardest to make a bunch of adolescents pay attention to a subject they had no interest in learning. Yes, becoming a teacher was not something Noelle had always wanted to do, but there she was. And whatever she did, she did to her very best.

The first day of the academic school year had begun that morning the same way it did most others—with a hot cup of coffee slowly steaming its alerting tendrils into her groggy brain, some parts of which were still very much asleep. People often forgot, she feared, that the prospect of returning to school after a long vacation was not just something loathed by the students, but by some teachers as well.

Staff meetings dragged on, lesson plans piled up, lists of curricula to be covered were handed out to each and every educator, and the academic year began anew.

She sat in the staffroom that morning, the first of the year, inhaling the scent of her latte with the determined vigor of an opium addict, and biting lightly at the nail of her right thumb. A particularly irritating member of staff from the Psychology department had been going on about the noise coming from the student common rooms at the end of the previous term for so long that even the beeping of the coffee machine in the corner had turned into a monotonous lullaby. Noelle watched the woman's pursed lips as they continued to complain, the pronounced lines around her mouth danced as the words poured on, etched by the twenty-a-day for the past twenty years.

"Morning, Noelle." She looked toward the familiar male voice, snapping her brain back into the room of caffeine fumes. Fraser Cole stood beside her, slowly swirling the bag of tea around and around in the large mug that was perched between his thick fingers.

"Good morning, Fraser." She took a gulp of her coffee as he sipped his tea. "Ready to be back?"

Her colleague raised a bushy eyebrow. "Back to the insanity of this place? Ready as I'll ever be. Had a paper jam already," he said, pointing to the mountain of photocopying that piled high on one of the surfaces in the corner of the room.

"That's the spirit, Fraser." Noelle patted him lightly on the shoulder and, still clutching her mug close to her chest, slipped as slyly as possible out of the staffroom.

To say Noelle enjoyed morning briefings would be a lie; to say that she tolerated them would also be pushing it slightly. It would be more accurate to say that she barely, and rarely, made it through an entire speech about what was and what was not an acceptable length of skirt, or the many reasons as to why it was vital to the school system that 'we all remove the capsule from the coffee machine after we're finished using it.' Yes, she listened to see if there were any notices of actual importance, and then escaped to her department office, where she was free to look over her hectic timetable and figure out what courses had to be completed for which years in the eternally limited time of each semester.

And to make this fresh academic year even more exciting, the department was one Math teacher down, and several students up. Oh, the joys. Of course, she was happy that Rachel Brooks—the youngest of the teachers in their department—had discovered that she was pregnant with her first child. However, what she was not so happy about was being informed three weeks before the beginning of the term that their already understaffed department was losing another pair of hands for the entire year.

Noelle sighed as the bell for her first class rang uncomfortably through her head. Grabbing a pile of papers from her desk—hoping that some of them were actually the ones she required—she got up, headed out of the department office, and into the classroom for the first time that year, the heavy fire door slamming shut behind her. A slam that reminded her that she was but at the starting line, with a long race ahead.

CHAPTER 3

"Did I ever mention my love for roses?" Phoenix twirled a long strand of hair between her thumb and forefinger, and looked up to the face of her therapist sitting opposite her.

She was back again, in that room where her brain was being dissected; each element of her mind and soul being dug out, picked apart, and put on show, as if she were a tomb of ancient secrets, and this woman was an archeologist searching for her piece of treasure. Too bad for the therapist that Phoenix wasn't filled with gold, just shattered pieces of pyrite that enticed people under a false pretense.

The woman smiled at her. That same, patronizing smile that she'd already learned to hate from their previous session. "No, I don't think you did."

Phoenix allowed her eyes to wander over the woman opposite her, trying to absorb every detail, trying to form a real human being out of the figure of hidden authority placed before her.

"Ever since I was a small child, roses have been something I've loved. I love the deep crimson color and the sweet smell that fills your nostrils when you sniff those vibrant petals. I love the thorns that sit so delicately on the side, completely harmless unless you pose a threat to the beauty of their stem... I don't see what there is not to love." Phoenix trailed off; her hazel eyes wandering over the pastel room until they settled on a particular scuff mark halfway up one of the walls. "That's what she reminded me of first."

"Roses?"

Phoenix nodded.

"And why is that?"

"The scent that emanated from her and floated around the room— it was roses."

"From Noelle?"

Phoenix nodded again.

"Light, floral. It's a smell that cleanses the senses." Phoenix paused. She could feel it coming again, that all too familiar sensation of her heart rising from her chest, into her throat, and trying to escape through her eyes. "And it reminded me of my mom's room."

"In the cottage?"

Phoenix sniffed, refusing to let the tears fall. "She'd always smelled like roses, too. Every time I walked into her bedroom, I'd be hit with the strong fragrance of her scented powders, and the little bottles that lined the wooden dresser... But that was a long time ago."

"How long ago did your mother die, Phoenix?"

"Eight years."

"And it was just you and your dad since then?"

"Yes, until he... Yes. Just me and dad." Phoenix paused. "She was beautiful, you know."

"Your mother?"

Phoenix nodded. "Yes. And so was Noelle. It was one of the first things I noticed."

"That she was pretty?"

"No no no," Phoenix shook her head and sat up straight in her seat. "I didn't say that. I mean, her eyes—god, her eyes!—were as an ocean, one full of interesting and wonderful things, just waiting to be explored. And the most intriguing shade of blue I have ever cared to notice. What I saw wasn't the sort of thing to come and go with age, and it wasn't the sort of aesthetic bullshit that's so often overly prized by *pretty* girls. I didn't say she was pretty; I said she was *beautiful*."

The therapist nodded slowly, her pen scribbling something on the pad that lay across her lap. Phoenix hated it when they did that. She hated that she couldn't see what was being written, what was being recorded about her, about whatever she'd said, perhaps even how she'd said it. Never before had she quite understood her father's paranoia when it came to mental health professionals, but she felt it now. She felt it full force.

"So," the therapist put down her pen, and pushed her glasses higher up on her nose, "let's go back to that first day again. What else do you recall?"

Phoenix shrugged. "Most of it, I guess. I walked through the corridors of the school building that morning, noting the seeming lack of people surrounding me, and I remember feeling instantly at peace."

"How so?"

"There's just something about being in a place that you know should be overly crowded, yet the absence of beings lets you feel as if you're not being concentrated on. As if the familiar place belongs only to you, and no one can take it away."

"Almost like a sense of ownership?"

"Almost like a sense of belonging."

The therapist nodded and scribbled something down in her secret little book. "What else?"

"I always enjoyed the time spent alone, to just sit and thrive in my own mind. Yet, it wasn't too long after this that my mind became an unsafe place to be. My usual happy and freeing thoughts were replaced, and though they were replaced with thoughts of an even greater nature, they hurt so much more to return from."

"And what else do you remember about that day at school?"

"The lesson itself is somewhat of a blur. Keeping a detailed record of my daily classes was never really a hobby of mine. Only the most notable moments that help one know what Is and Is Not ever stick in my brain. Always. Even when one isn't even aware that they're happening."

"Anything notable, then?"

"She walked in."

The therapist raised an eyebrow. "She walked in?"

"Oh, yes. It really was that simple."

There was a slight pause as the woman studied the young girl opposite her.

"Was there something in the way she walked in? Something that caught your attention?"

"She didn't exactly make a grand entrance if that's what you mean. It wasn't anything specifically memorable. It was normal, mundane. She sounded tired. But there was something in that, too. Something in her tone. A sort of hidden melody, one that held this peculiar power of calming me to a point where the words themselves seemed irrelevant. It didn't matter what she was saying, as long as she was saying it, and that I was there to listen."

"And that sound helped you to make a distinction between what Is and Is Not?"

"It was a sound I craved."

The therapist nodded slowly, her eyes doing something behind her glasses. Phoenix couldn't tell what exactly. A squint? A twitch? A flicker of doubt? She wasn't sure she cared.

"Oh! And that she was Not Miss Brooks," Phoenix almost guffawed. "I feel that the future would have turned out far differently had that not been the case. If only she had been Rachel Brooks and not Noelle Davis... then where would we be? Probably not Here, not Now. But Somewhere Else. Or, perhaps, just Nowhere."

"Nowhere? Like Juniper?"

Phoenix's face froze. Her mouth solidified into a hard line; her eyes still; her breath caught in her throat.

"Juniper was a good person," she said through gritted teeth, the tears welling in her eyes. "I had known her most of my life. She was more than just a friend; she was a sister. But we were different in many ways. There was a war in her mind, and she was the only one who could fight. And nothing anyone else could say or do would ever change that."

"It sounds like you cared for her very much. Would you like to talk more about what happened?"

Phoenix took a deep breath. "Juniper's childhood was far from easy. Most kids grow up with parents, be them one or two, who love and adore their child, who would give and take just to make sure their child was cared for and happy. But Juniper wasn't so lucky."

"It could definitely be said that your childhood wasn't easy either, Phoenix."

The young girl shook her head. "No, that was different. My mom *died*, and god knows that my dad was never really that stable. But they both loved me and did the best they could with what they had. And as for my dad, yeah, maybe it all got too much, but I don't blame him for what he did."

"That's a very interesting and forgiving way of seeing things."

"But it wasn't like that with Juniper. I still remember the day she opened up to me. The things she told me. The sickening things he'd done to her. It was awful, that harrowing sadness, the sadness of hearing about a love unrequited, a love to one's parents. One that was met with a different sort of love, and a different sort of touch." Phoenix trailed off, unable to prevent herself from being affected once more by the memory of that conversation.

"When did the two of you first meet?"

Phoenix thought for a moment. "When we were six years old. We met at school."

"And what were things like back then?"

"We were naïve, completely unaware of the Is and Is Nots of life."

The therapist sighed and moved her glasses from her eyes to rest atop her head. "You were only children, Phoenix."

"And yet how fast we were forced to grow. It was less than a year later that Juniper's parents were arrested."

"Why were her parents arrested?"

"A household domestic on a grand scale. A neighbor had heard the fracas coming from the house of the neighborhood junkies and called the cops. They found Juniper cowering in the yard. Her nose was bloody, and her arm was broken. I never really found out exactly what happened." She ran a hand throughout her chestnut hair as if the act of sweeping over her head would remove the cobwebs of memories from her mind. "I think that was when I saw the main similarities between Juniper and myself."

"And why do you think that is?"
"I'm not sure why, exactly. I mean, our situations were nothing alike," Phoenix shrugged her shoulders slightly, "but there was something in her eyes after that, something that gave away the feeling that we held in common."

"What feeling was that?

"The feeling of isolation. And yet I can't help but wonder that if I had said more, had done more, had shown her that she was not alone in this act of constant drowning, then perhaps she'd still be here today…"

The room fell silent for a moment. "I don't want to talk about this anymore."

"Okay," the therapist sighed, "we'll just put that aside for some other time, shall we? Now, going back to school. What else did you do on that first day?"

"I went home."

"And that's something that sticks in your mind as memorable that day? Going home?"

"Back to my little cottage down the lane. I arrived home that day and was met by echoing silence. From the sound of fumbling keys to the slamming of the door, the house just fell into a state of undisturbed quiet. And all I could do was stare."

"Stare at what?"

She shrugged. "Just stare. I stared at the lack of dishes piled in the sink. I stared at the cleanliness of the floors and walls. I stared at the perfect order of the bookshelf. I stared at all the things that were so different from how things had been Then. And, on that day, after being back at school, it was like it was hitting me for the very first time.

"I placed my keys in the previously unused dish by the door and walked along the short corridor to my room. My room was my haven, though it was also my prison. It was the one place I could run to in my house, where I could close the door, and never have to face the truth that lay outwith. But it was also a wall. A barrier between what Is and Is Not. And within the room, I found my bed and the full-length mirror to be my dearest friends. All the memories I hold of those two objects fill me up with sadness. The bed that took me to a million different places, taking the best of what I knew and bringing the promise of what Is and what Could Be in the darkest of night. And then the mirror, the first thing I saw in the sharp light of dawn, staring back at the reflection of myself and my world, bringing back the harsh reality of what Is Not."

The therapist furrowed her brow, readjusting her seating arrangements, fidgeting with her skirt as she moved her legs, her discomfort showing through. Phoenix was beginning to notice the cracks in her masque, becoming ever aware of the performance that went on before her. "Was this something that went through your head every morning?"

Phoenix nodded. "Juniper had scars, and so do I. Though scars, much like love, come in different forms. And my scars are not of the same nature as hers. Her skin showed the anger of parents long gone but never forgotten, and self-portraits telling tales of grief. Whereas my own are different. They aren't something physical that you can see on the surface. They're hidden, deep within my brain. Scars of memories and times past. Scars in the places where people used to be. Scars where those who are loved used to be."

CHAPTER 4

September 10th

You know, I've always had a way with numbers. I don't remember when it started, really, but ever since I was a small child, I've just had this natural ability to see solutions where others could not. Patterns are natural, they form everything around us—they are the air I breathe. There is something about the way digits work to complement each other, going around and around in this infinite cycle of pure logic; something about the reliability of the numerical system that I can look upon in nothing but awe and sheer amazement.

Perhaps it is this ability to recognize solutions that seems to draw people toward me. But how unfortunate it is for them that people are not numbers; they cannot be so easily solved.

Noelle put down her pen and sighed. She hadn't spent this much time thinking in a long while, and now that she was doing it, she realized that there had been a good reason for that. And it wasn't the reasons that she would so often give: that she was too busy, that there was always work to be done or people to see, that life didn't stop for anyone, and so what time did she have to just sit still and think? Yes, these things were a factor, of course, but the one true thing that Noelle had noticed since beginning this journaling exercise was that the main reason she didn't stop to think so deeply was simply that she didn't really want to. She didn't really want to dig around too much inside her mind because she was afraid of what she might find.

She breathed. Closing her eyes, she tried to concentrate her thoughts on something else, something better. And, taking another deep breath, she picked up her pen once more.

I met the man who was to become my dearest friend when I was at university. He always was an interesting specimen. I can still recall perfectly the first time I laid my eyes on this shaggy-haired eccentric, with his oversized checkered shirt that gave him the appearance of a lumberjack, and ripped bootleg jeans. Like he'd just stepped right out of The Breakfast Club. *Mark Stevens was the kind of man one might imagine as a high school dropout, a freelance artist, or maybe an up-and-coming musician of the alternative genre. But, in doing so, one would be wrong. Very wrong, indeed. Because, in fact, as hard as it may be to believe, Mark Stevens was one of the most brilliant minds in the country— the top physicist in the institution.*

People often said that Mark looked more like a drug addict than a physicist, and as much as it breaks my heart to admit, they wouldn't have been entirely wrong.

The day they met was one Noelle would carry with her until the day she died. Though she was not sure why, exactly: it wasn't overly eventful, no large-scale incidents of love or loathing took place, and she would almost have been tempted to say that it was just a normal day, completely lacking life-changing events. Almost. But that's the thing—as mundane and extremely ordinary as it may be, she supposed the happenings of that day did change her life. It's a funny thing, how each normal passing day can seem so much like nothing, and yet when one puts it all together, suddenly a lifetime is formed, seemingly out of nowhere. And yet, looking back, she could see that although nothing jumped into line to change her whole direction, maybe it did set the wheels in motion for everything that came next.

Everything she'd ever loved; everything she'd ever lost.

Noelle had been standing in line outside the registrar's office on her first day of higher education. Eighteen years old and greener than the hills that line Elk Valley, she had no idea how she was supposed to navigate this whole wide world she'd been thrust into. Everything was new and confusing, and it had dawned on her earlier that day that she didn't actually know where it was she was supposed to be going to get to her first lecture. And so, there she found herself, standing in a queue of people who were all just as new and confused as she. And it was there that he found her.

"Excuse me." The first time Noelle heard his voice was from behind. As she stood in the queue that ran out of the office, coffee cup in one hand, books in the other, she was completely oblivious to the world that didn't consist of a seemingly infinite number of people standing in front of her—when she had such a numbered time in which for them to disappear—and due to such, she didn't even see where he had come from.

One minute he wasn't there, the next he was.

"Are you gonna drink that?" Noelle turned to look up at the man whose index finger was pointed toward the cup in her hand. Dark hair flew in curls down to his stubble-lined jaw, a tattered leather jacket hung from his shoulders, and a pair of gray fingerless gloves sheathed his large hands. Noelle looked from the man to her coffee, and back to the man again.

"Um," she hesitated, unsure of how to respond, and gave him just enough time to pinch the cup from her grasp.

"Thanks," he winked, before starting off speedily in the opposite direction, taking her drink with him.

"Hey!" Noelle had called after him, but it was too late, he was gone.

In the time it had taken for her to have her morning lifeline stolen, the queue in which she was waiting had moved down substantially, and it wasn't much later that she found herself pushing open the door to her first lecture on mathematics in university. She entered the hall quickly and found a seat, carefully placing her pens and paper so that she would be able to comfortably take the most detailed notes of her life. She heard the lecturer enter before she saw him, and she couldn't believe her ears.

"Morning everyone," Noelle looked up as he strode into the center of the room, her cup of coffee still held in his left hand, "my name is Professor Mark Stevens."

•••

Noelle thought back to this moment as she looked down at the latte from the cafeteria machine in front of her and smiled.

"What do you think, Noelle?" The familiar sound of Fraser's voice brought her back to her surroundings, back to the rabble of the school lunch hall, and all the things she should be doing, despite the many, many other thoughts she had whirring around in that busy brain of hers. Things to write in the journal when she got home, she supposed.

"Sorry, what?" Noelle had not been listening.

"The History field trip next Tuesday, we still need staff chaperones."

"Oh," she sighed, registering the mundane conversations that had become her life in these last four years. "Sorry, I can't. The Math department is worryingly understaffed and over-student-ed this year."

Fraser smiled at her sympathetically. "That's fine, I know you're busy."

And that was it; that was exactly the way she could be described: she was busy. Yes. But as much as she seemed to have all of her time filled to the brim with marking assignments, organizing classes and curricula, restocking supplies, and overseeing other department members, there was still this feeling that she couldn't shake. This feeling of harrowing emptiness that overwhelmed her the minute she closed the door to her apartment every evening, the great echoing silence that rushed unto her the second she placed her keys on the hook by the door, the realization that made nothing about the life she lived seem very real at all.

And there she was again: alone, in an empty apartment, wondering what to do with herself. Praying that she would realize more of her evening than spending it exactly the same way as she had every other; hoping that writing in that goddamn journal wasn't going to end up being the highlight of her night, just because it was something new.

It was a peculiar feeling that gathered in her each night she returned; it was as if she was a stranger in her own home. Like the very walls and surfaces of the place she lived weren't really hers at all; like everything around her was alien and unfamiliar; like she'd just stepped aimlessly into a world she'd never seen before.

But then Noelle would take some more small steps, farther into the corridor of this living space, deeper into this odd collection of surroundings, and suddenly it wasn't so odd anymore—it was just her apartment.

Noelle would place her things from work on the sofa, like every night. She would turn on the TV, more for the sound of voices than for what they were saying, like every night. She would switch on the lights in her kitchen and get down to concocting from various organic ingredients a meal for one, like every single other night of her adult human existence. And then what would she do? Sit on her sofa in her warm living room; watch TV, the news, some documentaries; grade pages after pages of amateur mathematics; and drink a glass of wine. Then, sometime later, she would crawl into the soft embrace of her half-empty double bed, and lay awake for hours, drifting in and out of sleep until morning. When it would start all over again.

Don't misunderstand the situation; Noelle believed firmly that her life was perfectly okay. She had a house, and a stable job, and there were always people around her. She would meet up with friends on weekends for the occasional drink and often find herself sitting at a table with one sibling or the other for a midweek meal. But she still felt this cruel want to fill some sort of gaping hollowness that rumbled through her soul.

So, where did that leave her? Looking at her life, the routines that appeared to form its entire structure, the monotone repetition of daily bumbling. It all just seemed so superficial, so meaningless, so paltry.

And that was the bottom line; as much as everything was perfectly okay, Noelle was still desperately unhappy.

CHAPTER 5

Phoenix entered the room that was becoming increasingly familiar to her. She was sure it would only take her one or possibly two more sessions before she gained the ability to map out the whole office. From the exact positioning of the chairs, to the desk under the window at the end of the room; from each individual mark on the floor, to the little bumps of air that speckled the paint on the walls; from the clock whose hands ticked away the moments of her life, to the fine layers of dust that gathered on the folders sitting on the shelf.

"You don't seem very happy, Phoenix," the therapist looked up at the girl sitting across from her. "Is there any reason for that?"

The young patient flickered her eyes up to the woman who was facing her and gave nothing but a blank stare in response. "Is there any reason I should be happy?"

The doctor shrugged. "You tell me."

Phoenix sighed. It was difficult to think of reasons why she should be happy, but she also knew that there were still many things in her life that she should be grateful for. Like the hope of the future, like all of the plans that she could make, like the things she could possibly achieve, and who she could potentially one day become. And she was painfully aware that not everyone had these opportunities. Not anymore.

"I don't know," she replied at last. "I feel very out of place."

"It's perfectly natural to have that response given that you've just been placed in foster care. I know it's tough to adjust, and you've been through a lot, not just in the last year but also in general. It's normal to feel out of place at first." There was a pause. "You know Phoenix, sometimes it can help to stay active in hobbies and interests. Is there anything you like to do?"

Phoenix thought for a moment. "When I was younger, I liked to bake."

"And why was that?"

"I don't think I've ever really figured out why; I was never any good at it."

The therapist adjusted her glasses. "And why do you say that?"

The girl gave a light laugh. "My cupcakes were always burned, my scones rock hard, my cakes would never rise—but, for some reason, I enjoyed it nonetheless. My mom and I would spend hours in the kitchen, working away, creating weird and wonderful things;

mine being the weird, of course, and my mom's being the wonderful. My mom always used to decorate her cupcakes with edible rose petals. Perhaps that's another reason as to why I love them so. We would go from the kitchen through to the lounge, where my father would be waiting with a smile on his face, his glasses perched at the end of his nose, and he would take a bite. His face always lit up after that, as he went on to compliment how my skills were always *coming along smoothly*."

Phoenix stopped for a moment, the corners of her mouth twitching at a smile as the memory played. But it was quickly followed by that familiar feeling in her chest; the one that felt like her heart was going to explode and caused her eyes to burn as tears welled within them. "And I would giggle with glee, completely captivated by the sounds of his sweet lies. After all, what else would be expected from a six-year-old girl?"

It was then that her voice failed her, cracking with the words that she said, as hot tears began to roll down her cheeks. She said softly, "But that was Then. And this is Now."

A silence descended upon the room as the therapist allowed Phoenix a few moments to gather herself, before once again beginning her line of questioning.

"Let's talk about something else," began the therapist, softly. "When did things start changing at school?"

Phoenix reflected on the question for a second, pushing the

memories of the far past back to their respective places in her brain. "It wasn't until November that I first noticed it."

"Noticed what?"

"I don't know exactly…" she trailed off and shook her head lightly. "Perhaps it was nothing really, just a little preference. It was as if I was starting to see her a little more. And maybe it was at that point that I decided that I kind of liked her. As if after three months of not thinking about it, months of just walking around in a kind of haze, going from task to task, wandering through life like I was in a daydream, something penetrated my subconscious. And I guess that's when I decided that I liked her."

"And why is that? Why do you think that after these months you took a preference, took a notice? When before, as you've said, you were quite indifferent to the world?"

Phoenix smiled lightly. "It was her personality that hooked me first. And not the deeper regions of it—which I was to find out later—but the basic signs that told people, that told *me*, who she was."

The therapist nodded slowly. "And who was that?"

"That's not my place to say," Phoenix faltered, unsure how to continue.

The therapist crossed her legs once more and placed her left arm loosely over the chair where she sat. "Okay. But what did these thoughts, or perhaps this realization, mean to you?"

Phoenix thought for a moment.

"It gave me something; something to hold onto, something new in my life." Phoenix sighed. "But the month that I was given something new, so was Juniper."

"What was that?"

"The writing on the wall."

"Hmm," the therapist put her notepad to one side and nonchalantly placed a hand upon her chin. "Tell me more."

Phoenix chewed at the corner of her lips. A large part of her still didn't want to talk about this, but here she was, and her attendance was mandatory. So, why not speak the truth?

•••

That day, Phoenix met up with Juniper outside the cafeteria. Even from down the hallway as Juniper approached, Phoenix could tell she was in a good mood. Many others would not have seen the difference in her face, but then again, many others didn't know her as Phoenix did. She was a foreign text, was Juniper; before you could read the book, you first had to learn the language.

From her distance, Phoenix could see it—a smile in her eyes. And as she approached her, the smile in her eyes moved to create a smile on her pierced lips.

"Phoenix!" she yelled with an undeniable sense of glee. "You'll never guess what happened this morning!"

She was right; Phoenix never would have guessed, so she simply shrugged.

Juniper then proceeded to do her usual when excited, and tell Phoenix everything at a hundred miles per hour. "So, I was in History a few weeks ago and this guy was, like—Oh my god, this guy! He's so amazing!—He was like, *so you're hot wanna go on a date?* And I was like, *Yes!* And then we had this date and then another and another, then on Saturday—ah! It was so good!"

"Right..." Phoenix looked at her friend for a while, her facial contortions seemingly failing in their task of portraying her complete lack of understanding in what had just been said to her. "All I heard was something about a guy and a date."

"Yeah!" Juniper yelped, grabbing Phoenix's shoulders and shaking her in excitement, while the chestnut-haired girl ground her teeth and waited for the localized earthquake to stop.

Apparently, she'd been dating this boy for a few weeks, and on their last date, he had named her as his girlfriend. Officially. Phoenix was pleased for her, and she showed it by matching her excitement, discussing what she should wear for seeing him, and by nudging her whenever she saw him looking at them in a hallway. It was the norm for any teenager, but Phoenix had other things on her mind. Things that not even Juniper could understand. Things that Phoenix herself didn't even understand.

•••

"It was weird," Phoenix exhaled. "It was as we sat down to eat lunch that I saw her; Ms. Davis, that is—being the Math teacher who is *not* Miss Brooks—as she walked into the room."

"Why is that weird?" inquired the therapist.

"Because it was then that I experienced something strange. I remember that my eyes followed her as she queued, watching her as she picked up her food, and placed it carefully on her tray, looking on as she sat down beside other teachers from her department..." The young girl shook her head lightly. "That's weird, right? That I would even remember that. And in those lost moments of looking at that which Is Not, I had managed to miss most of what Juniper had been saying about her new relationship. And it occurred to me that I had missed what was Said due to something that was Said Not. How strange this world is... "

"Hmm," the therapist mused, tapping her pen against the page of the notepad that was sitting open again upon her lap. "Did those become common thoughts?"

"The following few weeks were pretty much the same. I would catch myself looking at her as she walked around the building, or thinking about her at the most random of times. I found myself actively looking forward to our lessons, and the feeling of disappointment when she wasn't there became something I actually noticed. I would simply be scanning a crowd, and a part of me would automatically start searching for her. I can't say why. I don't know why." She sighed heavily and rubbed a hand over her head. "And I can't believe *that's* what I was thinking about when I should have been paying more attention to Juniper."

"Why do you say that? The situation you described earlier didn't seem so bad," commented the therapist. "But tell me how you viewed it."

Phoenix sighed; it was hard to explain. "I loved to see her happy. There was something about seeing a smile that had endured so much pain, which gave me strength. And knowing just how much pain this particular girl had lived through, and to still have the honor of sharing in these mini moments of bliss, was something that filled me not only with a little bit of brightness but also with a deep sense of pride for her. Pride in knowing what Juniper had been through, and how much she had overcome. I was proud to be her friend.

"But there is one particular memory, which I still carry with me. One I often find pushing its way into my brain at the most unwarranted moments."

"And what is that?"

"It was a day when we were in Middle School. December. There was a river in the middle of the forest clearing that was situated not far from Juniper's foster home, and we thought that it would be a good place to escape, where the other kids wouldn't come at that time of year," Phoenix began. "We were often adventuring out on our own, finding little unknown hovels around the place, where we could set our foundations and hide from everyone else. We were walking by the banks, leaving our tracks in the snow, before spying the small stone bridge that moved across the ice below…" she trailed off.

A few moments of silence followed.

This is why Phoenix did not like therapy; it meant talking about things that she would rather remain Said Not, dragging skeletons out of dark cupboards, reliving things that she wished she had never lived in the first place. Things that were too much to live through even once and were not desired to be brought up again.

"You've gone blank," the therapist commented. "Do you remember what you were going to say?"

"I remember it," Phoenix sighed, "but when I think back, my thoughts begin to tangle, and I become confused."

"Do you think you can try to tell me?"

Phoenix took a deep breath. "To recall the day is easy, but to recall what happened, what *really* happened, is far more difficult. The events seem to alter slightly every time I think about it. The reasons *why* altering even more."

"Why do you think that is?"

"Because I don't think I ever did know. Not really. I have an idea, I have a few, but I fear the truth of it may be hidden forever. A miniature kink in the eternal spiral of time, continually receding until it is lost in the dark abyss. And yet I'll never forget it, the chill that blew through the late December air; the cold that nipped at our hands, feet, and noses, turning them red in the evening glow; the delicate snowflakes that fell upon them, keeping our senses aware. These things I can recall. These things never change."

The therapist readjusted her position, crossing her legs and sitting upright in her chair. "Tell me more about it."

"The bridge was slippery beneath our feet, and to reach the apex of the arched stoned structure proved more of a struggle than intended. But soon we found ourselves at the climax, looking out across the forest that surrounded us. Great white pines swayed gently in the light breeze, causing little caster sugar snowfalls around the covered forest floor. I remember that Juniper turned her head from the vast mass of trees that had caught my attention and changed her view to that of the world beneath us. I remember her looking at the faint swirl of water trapped beneath the hard, outer case of dusted ice; the little bits of frost sparkling in the bluish glow from the hidden sun, as they danced across the surface.

And that's when it happened."

"When what happened?"

"You know, I still thank whatever god may be listening that things ended the way they did that day. I remember watching in confusion as Juniper placed her ungloved hands atop the white wall, thinking only how cold she must be making her fingers, sliding pale skin along the frigid stone. I watched as she gathered her strength, and with a little hop, heaved her body to sit upon it." Phoenix paused for a minute. "There was a moment then; one where Juniper had looked deeply into my eyes, and all I could do was stare back. Sapphire and hazel, locked in a gaze of what is Said Not. And then… well, then things get hazy."

"How so?"

"I'm not sure how Juniper got from sitting atop the wall, to Not, but somehow she did. I've played the scenario over and over again, trying to remember how, but I can't. Did she slip? Did she lose her balance? Was she trying to reach for a falling snowflake? Or did she just lie back? I never knew. A part of me doesn't truly want to know. It's all very well to say, or even just to think, such things, to play out different scenarios over in one's head. But it's pointless, really. Because, often, the reality of the situation is that we don't want to know, for the fear that we cannot bear the truth." Phoenix rubbed her temple, pressing her fingertips into the side of her head as if there were a button that she could reach in there that would switch off the pain. "But at the end of the day, does the reason why really matter? It doesn't change anything. It doesn't change what happened."

"And what did happen, Phoenix?"

The young girl brought her hand down from her head and began to bite lightly at her nails.

"I'll never forget the sound of ice cracking as Juniper's pale body collided with the frozen wastes below. I remember sticking my head over the wall just in time to see her figure disappear into a swirl of icy water... I don't really know how I did what I did next. Another gap in my memory, I suppose. All I know is that, somehow, I got her out."

"You got her out?" This time the therapist looked surprised, the first real emotion that Phoenix had been able to gauge from their sessions. "How did you do that?"

"Thinking back, I must've jumped in after her. Because the next thing I remember is pushing my way through the stabbing pain of a liquid that felt more as if it were made of acid than of ice. I vaguely recall spying Juniper's naturally black locks of her childhood suspended just below the surface, and scrambling toward her, trying my best to ignore the clenching cold that had wrapped itself around my legs and lungs."

"Wow, Phoenix," the doctor shook her head lightly, "that's quite a thing to have done, especially at such a young age. It's rather heroic, really."

"It wasn't heroic, she was my best friend," Phoenix replied instantly, and then went silent for a moment, her mind seeming to have suddenly hit a mental block, a wall trying to protect her from what lay in wait on the other side.

The therapist noticed this; she could see it in the way the young girl's strikingly bronze eyes glazed over. But in order to this to work, for her sessions to have effect, the wall must be broken down.

"Go on," she prompted in a calm monotone.

"When we reached the icy banks Juniper was unconscious, and I didn't know what to do. Heroes always know what to do."

"I'm not sure that's true, Phoenix. I think maybe heroes question things as well, sometimes. So, what did you do?"

"I ran as fast as I could back to town and found help."

This time it was the therapist who sighed. "That's quite extraordinary, Phoenix. I can only imagine how cold you must have been, how much you must have ignored your own body, considering that you, too, had been in that water. It really does say something about your character."

Phoenix snorted. "Oh yeah? What does it really say about my character? That I was a good friend? That I did what I thought was best? That I was stupid to attempt something so dangerous? Because I don't know what to think. All I know is that there was something about that feeling. Something about being almost numb. It felt unreal, as If I were a bird trying to run when what I needed was to fly."

The room fell silent once again as both contained within thought over the conversation that had just taken place. The therapist thinking over all that Phoenix had just told her, what it showed about her, what it meant, how it could've potentially impacted the way things were Now. While Phoenix saw it differently, remembering the story almost as if it had happened to someone else.

"So," the therapist broke the silence, "how was this resolved?"

Phoenix shrugged. "I got help. I took them to Juniper. I told them she'd fallen through the ice whilst we were playing. How else could I have explained what really happened, when I wasn't even exactly sure myself? And after that, Juniper was taken to the hospital and treated for hypothermia, as was I. Her foster parents came as soon as they heard, and my dad came for me."

"That's quite an ordeal, Phoenix. How did you feel about all of that?"

"I was happy that people came for Juniper, and that she got to go home."

"Do you think it was a good place for her? Is that why you are happy that she got to go home?"

"I'd been to Juniper's home a few times. I rather liked it. Her foster parents were nice, and although the house itself was rather rundown, it wasn't as bad as some. In the Golding household, there were many children. Most orphaned, some only placed in temporary custody, some adopted. But Juniper didn't really socialize with any of them."

"Are there any other kids in your foster home?" Phoenix shook her head. "And do you know how Juniper felt about her situation?"

"She didn't mind it there, though she didn't get much attention. As the oldest of the children under their roof, Juniper was left mainly to do as she pleased, while Mr. and Mrs. Golding had their hands full with the other children.

"They never asked anything of her, and sometimes I wonder if she may have been better off if they had. I think that Juniper may have needed something to occupy her time, something to keep her from the darkness of her own mind. Something to bring her into the present world, and out of the shadows of her past."

The therapist nodded slowly once again, an action that Phoenix was becoming so accustomed to that she could almost time it. Starting at the reaction time from whatever she'd said, to the number of seconds that the nodding continued. "Do you ever feel like that?"

"Juniper and I were very different people. And I always felt as if I should have been able to do more. But at the end of the day, we each receded to two different worlds. Worlds that only we could see."

CHAPTER 6

September 12^{*th*}

Not many people have a favorite planet, but I do. I'm not sure why; I just do. It's Jupiter, in case you may be wondering. Why Jupiter? Well, I love how grand it is, I love how its mass is two and a half times that of all the other planets in the solar system combined. I love how it gives the illusion of something so solid, even though it's not. Not at all, actually. In fact, it's just a large ball of gas with a few rocky components somewhere in the center, and that's amazing, really, how despite its vast size and imposing view, it's just as hollow as the rest of us.

When I was a kid, my father would take me to the science center, and we'd spend whole days looking at all the wondrous things the universe had to offer. We'd walk through rows upon rows of charts and diagrams, pretty pictures of patterns so complex that a child, such as myself, could do nothing but gape at how marvelous it all was. Especially when my father would lift me up to see the details of the large maps that I couldn't ever hope to view from my three and a half feet, and point to that small blue dot in the loops of an intricate solar system, and say:

"See that, Ellie? That's Earth—where we are, right now." *Then he'd ruffle his large hands through the naturally dusty brunette locks that prevailed throughout my childhood and smile down at me with pride.*

And I would crinkle my nose and refuse to accept that we lived in such a miniature and insignificant-looking dot, pointing instead to that large gas giant, which looked so much more appealing to my five-year-old ambition to dominate the galaxy.

Noelle sighed as she looked at the words on the page, the scribbles of ink that brought back her childhood. She remembered rather a lot about her younger years and often thought of that early time with fondness. Before the world grabbed ahold of her and threw her into the whirlwind that was to become her life. If only she'd been able to retain more of that five-year-old girl in her brain.

Such ambition; such wasted energy.

Don't get me wrong, I think ambition is a wonderful thing, something to be encouraged and nurtured so that one day it is no longer ambition, but fact, life; the way things are, as opposed to what they could potentially be. But sometimes it just doesn't work out, and suddenly all that time, that planning, that hope, just disintegrates right in front of your eyes.

I don't really remember my father living at home, though at times—perhaps when I'm conversing with my brother, or sitting through one of my mother's rambling speeches—I find that I am niggled by fragments of nonspecific memories, pushing lightly from the corners of my mind, trying to make me recall days long gone by. However, aside from our trips to the science center, a day I will never forget is the one during which I was first introduced to Valeriya.

Noelle and her younger sister had been sitting on the sofa in their grandmother's house one lazy Sunday afternoon, her brother perched on the floor with a pack of playing cards. Noelle believed she had been reading a book about something—most likely one of the biographies of great scientists that often occupied the free hours of her early life—while her sister entertained herself with unrelenting bouncing on the end of the sofa, when their father entered the room with a strange woman on his arm.

The sight of this new body was just peculiar enough for her sister to cease her acrobatic activities, and stare with a composed picture of confusion as daddy dearest approached his three beloved children. Noelle placed her book down on her lap as her brother put his playing cards to one side. The figure of her grandmother appeared from the kitchen and stood in the doorway behind their father, and she remembered wondering why the old woman looked the way she did as she lightly wrung her hands.

"Jack, Ellie, Kirsten," their father looked at them individually, and motioned to the woman by his side, who took a step forward, "this is Valeriya. She's going to be your new stepmother."

Now, I can't accurately say what the feeling was, exactly, that ran its way deep into my young mind that day, but I'm sure my siblings felt it, too. It was some sort of bewilderment, some sort of bitterness, some sort of... betrayal? I don't know; I was only a child. And this woman was a stranger; a stranger that I was now expected to treat as a mother.

Noelle stopped suddenly, lifting her hand away from the lined page as if it had suddenly gone up in flames. She couldn't figure out what had just happened, how her mind had jumped subjects so quickly, so unwarranted, so out of the blue. A minute ago, she was thinking about her childhood, about her father, about how things had changed... And now she was thinking about Phoenix—how had that happened? She put the pen back to paper.

It's a strange thing to remember, and I'm not really sure why it's come into my brain. Maybe that's what the journaling does; maybe it's meant to bring up seemingly random things, maybe just to make us think about them. But there was a conversation, almost a year ago. It wasn't even really anything. I'd asked her how she was, and although I wasn't entirely convinced that I believed what she said, I let her be. After all, what business was it of mine to intrude upon her life? I'm just a middle-aged woman who teaches grumpy kids for cash, what could I possibly have done? What could I ever have done?

●●●

It was as they were approaching the bittersweet relief of the winter break that Noelle first noticed something that, for some odd reason, hadn't been able to leave her mind since. The first class of the morning rolled on as they all did; teenagers aimlessly strolled in through the door, equations went up on the board, textbooks were opened, and brains began to shift slowly into gear for the day ahead. Noelle was not sure what it was that made her look in her direction that day, but by whatever twist of fate, she just happened to glance down at the first table in front of her desk—please note that the fact that she hardly ever did this was not due to an ignorance of the student there, but simply because of the coincidental placement of files, of books, of things too close to be seen.

Noelle remembered fixing her eyes upon this student at the front of her class, and noticing the waxen pallor of her youthful skin; seeing the contrast of a hundred sleepless years in her eyes; being witness to that aspect in her demeanor that spoke so true to that of her own—that same emptiness.

"Miss Hudson, are you all right?" Even as Noelle said the words, she felt her eyebrows crinkle beyond her control. The girl looked up at her as though realizing where she was for the first time.

"I—" she began, coughing lightly. "I'm fine."

"Are you sure?" Noelle asked, unable to keep herself from becoming more attuned to this unusual familiarity she could sense emanating from the young girl. "You look a bit pale."

"Yeah. I'm good."

And that was it.

Christmas hurtled into Noelle's life as quickly that year as it did any other, and it was once again time for her annual family get-together. She thought of this as if it were a rare occurrence, when in fact it was nothing of the sort. She often saw her siblings for midweek meals and weekend drinks, but the difference during this particular holiday was that they were all together in the same place, at the same time—even their mother.

From the back seat of the taxi, Noelle watched as the car crawled slowly toward the gray-paneled building in suburbia, watching as the long hedgerows began to gap intermittently, giving passers-by little glimpses into the lives of the street's residents. Enabling them the view of delicately decorated trees, elegantly equipped light displays, and kitsch commodities clinging to door and window frames.

Children could be viewed through the small portals into the world of the middle-class, frolicking around on the morning of their favorite holiday, hoping to get the parents to allow them to rip into the presents that lay strewn under the tree.

But the cab rolled past these painted portraits of the ideal childhood and came to a stop outside the home of Noelle's younger sister. She handed her cash to the driver and stepped out onto the street, listening as the wheels screeched lightly against the snow as the vehicle sped off to pick up another body with family to see this Christmas, with things to do or places to be. For a moment she just stood there, looking over at the front door, the wreath nailed to the wood above the knocker, taking in the obvious show of festivity expressed by the seasonal adornments lining the house's exterior.

"Noelle!" Her sister extended her arms wide as she opened the door. "Merry Christmas!"

"Merry Christmas, Kirsten," Noelle smiled, embracing her younger sibling.

"Noelle!" Their mother ran over to her as she entered the lounge, wrapping her arms around her. "Merry Christmas, love."

"Merry Christmas, mom," Noelle replied, squeezing her lightly. And in the corner of the room, she could see Jack—a green cracker crown sitting upon his brow—smiling slyly at her, drink in hand.

"Jackie!" she laughed, approaching her brother with open arms.

"Good god, Elle," he chuckled, "don't ever call me that again."

"Aw, but it's Christmas! Can't drop it now, if only for the sake of tradition," she flashed him a grin, her tongue placed firmly between her front teeth.

That was the peculiar thing about this particular holiday; it had this universal (and yet still slightly unusual) way of bringing people together. Although, Noelle knew perfectly well that this isn't always the case. In fact, she recalled almost perfectly the first Christmas they had spent in the company of their father and his new Russian bride.

As they all sat down at the table that year, they were each presented with a card. Noelle's featured a polar bear wearing a blue toque, who appeared to be calling 'round at some neighboring igloo to ask if they would 'care to talk about Jesus.' It read:

> *Dear Noelle,*
> *I wish you a warm Christmas and a happy new year!*
> *With love,*

Валерия

Taking her index finger, she traced it over the foreign figures, feeling the newness of the interesting characters beneath her touch. She'd heard the woman speaking her mother tongue on the phone a few times by then, but Noelle had never envisaged the stark difference of the language she spoke, the way it was written, the alien meanings behind the phrases that have no distinguishable translation. To this day, she was still not entirely sure whether it was simply the way in which her brain processed information that made this such a difficult aspect of this woman to understand, or whether it was the deep-seated astringency that had slowly coiled its way into her heart from their first meeting.

Noelle learned a lot about her father as she grew up. When she was a kid, he seemed perfect: always teaching, loving, raising her to the top of the world. He was a hero in Noelle's eyes, and nothing could convince her otherwise. But as she aged it was as if someone had lifted the veil, and suddenly she saw him for what he really was—a regular human being, full of faults, and holding a record of monumental mistakes. Valeriya, she felt, was one of these mistakes. She already had a mother, and as unhinged as she could occasionally become, Noelle never entertained the idea of replacing her.

Once the evening of festivities had reached its conclusion, and Noelle had said her farewells to her mother and siblings, she returned to the familiar esotericism of her apartment. After exchanging her Sunday best for the comfort of her pajamas, Noelle soon found herself going through the tedious task of her nighttime routine. She stared at her tired reflection looking back at her as she rubbed off her make-up, revealing the wrinkles that had begun to creep out from the corner of her eyes in recent years. Turning the tap, she let the water run in the hopes of it reaching a reasonably warm temperature as she brushed her teeth.

And there was that feeling again. The one she couldn't quite put her finger on; the one that left her chest heaving; the one that reminded her of the reality of her solitary abode. She watched as the view of her doppelgänger blurred through the steam rising from the sink, saving her the humiliation of watching on as tears began to drip from her chin.

CHAPTER 7

"Did I ever mention my love for ladybugs?" Phoenix twirled a finger through a lock of long dark hair as she sat in her usual seat in the therapist's office.

The woman smiled back at her. "No, I don't think that's something we've discussed."

"Hmm," sighed Phoenix, a slight smile twitching at her lips. "Ladybugs. I've always held a respect for ladybugs."

"And why is that?

The young girl shrugged. "I don't really know why. Perhaps, like the roses, it's their rich crimson color, or maybe their sweet little spots. Or maybe their ability to be liked by most humans, as opposed to hated for being a pesky insect. Maybe it's their useful nature of eating aphids, one in which they feed off other living creatures, but are accepted for it due to its greater good. Perhaps it's all these things, but the thing that I love most is quite simply that they can fly."

The therapist thought about this for a moment. "Many things can fly, Phoenix. So, I wonder, what is it about these particular bugs that makes you like them better than, say, a blue jay?"

Phoenix shrugged again. "I think maybe it's the way they wander in a fashion seemingly aimless. Using their tiny little legs to climb heights not seen by humans. And then when they feel the need to escape, they gracefully extend their tiny wings, and flutter off into the distance, most likely never to be seen again." She laughed. "If only human life were that simple."

The therapist nodded slowly, doing that thing she did where she paused for a moment, seemingly taking in the information from her patient, storing it all away in that brain of hers. She then took the little booklet from her desk and flicked through a few pages, before looking back up at the girl sitting across from her. "I am led to believe that winter was particularly difficult for you, is that true?"

Phoenix mumbled. "You can say that again."

"Can you tell me what happened?"

"Yes," Phoenix said flatly.

•••

It was a day near Christmas when things changed. The previous night had been one of considerable difficulty. Phoenix had returned from school that evening, greeted by the usual silent darkness of her lifeless house, and after dropping her keys in the dish, reached for the light switch. She flicked the switch with her finger and waited. Nothing. She flicked it a few more times. Still nothing.

It was then that an awful thought washed over her. With a groan, she turned on her heels and headed out to the mailbox. And there it was—the little white envelope, sitting so innocently within the rusting metal box. It was from the electricity board.

They had shut them off. Or, more accurately, they had shut *her* off. Phoenix was the only one left. She sighed heavily and began searching through drawers for any candles she might find to light her soulless home. It wasn't until she'd finished running around finding and lighting candles that she noticed the heating had been shut off as well.

Phoenix walked slowly to her bedroom and sat on her cold duvet. She thought she could do it. At fifteen, she thought she'd be old enough to live alone. But it was hard. She hadn't realized that before. She thought she would manage fine. But that was before everything her father had already paid had run out. That was when she was still living off what he'd left behind. That was before the reality of what Is finally hit her.

She was alone. Her mother was dead; her father was gone. Where he'd gone was another of those things she didn't think she'd ever know. She'd walked through to the kitchen one morning in July to see a note left on the counter. The scratchy words not quite seeming to be written in a language she could understand, and yet, somehow, she knew what it meant. He was never coming back.

•••

"How did you know?"

Phoenix looked up at the therapist as she interrupted her line of thought. "How did I know what?"

"That he was never coming back."

Phoenix sighed. "He always struggled since the death of my mother. My dad's schizophrenic, you see, and things got a lot worse when she left us…"

•••

Dirty dishes sat piled up in the sink for weeks. Bits of half-finished paintings scattered the halls. Blotches of paint speckled every surface. Classical music could be heard from everywhere in the small cottage. Phoenix would often hear him talking to it, responding to the music that seemingly told him what to do. But that was Then. Once he left, she cleaned and things stayed clean. The paintings were all ordered and placed in the spare room, the one where he had been sleeping since her mother died. The paint was locked away in cupboards. The cottage was silent.

It didn't have to be silent. Phoenix stood from her bed and grabbed the violin that sat beside her mirror. She made her way back along the corridor, and as she reached the middle door on her left, she stopped. Placing her hands against the cool of glossed wood, she pushed it open.

The strong scent hit her as soon as she entered, pushing its invisible tendrils into her nose, and infecting her brain with images from the past. Phoenix closed the door behind her, to make sure that none of the smell escaped. Roses. She started toward the great mahogany bed and perched upon the pastel pink comforter. Gently, she lifted the instrument to her neck and placed her chin upon it. Bow in hand, she closed her eyes and began pulling it against the strings, letting the classics poor around the small cottage once more.

Phoenix didn't know how long she played. But once her eyelids began to close, she knew it was time to place the violin and bow to one side. She woke up still atop the covers of her mother's bed the next morning. 08:00. She was late.

She was the first person Phoenix saw that day—Ms. Davis, that is.

After fleeing from the buried memories of her mother's room—careful to make sure the door was fully closed as she left—she quickly gathered her things for the day and ran from the house, still dressed in the clothes she'd fallen asleep in the night before.

She was sitting in her class that morning, the first one of the day, which really did make her the first person she'd seen since the previous night. Well, aside from the shades that twinkled at the corner of her eyes everywhere she went. The shades of those who were supposedly human. But to Phoenix, they were just shades; shadows in her vision that never conversed with her world. Instead, they just talked to each other, in their strange ghostly tongues, and never took notice of the living as she walked on by.

Thirty minutes had gone by before Ms. Davis turned to her. To say Phoenix was surprised would be an understatement; she was absolutely amazed. She hadn't thought she could see her behind the walls—hers made of paper and files; Phoenix's made of ring binders and blurred lines, mixed up with doodles of ladybugs climbing up thin stalks. For a minute, she doubted if it was even her that she was actually looking at. Perhaps her gaze had just shifted toward Phoenix's general direction. Phoenix did that sometimes, looked like she was staring at something or someone, when, in fact, she was somewhere else entirely.

But no. Ms. Davis really was looking at her, eye contact and all. Her great river rushing to join Phoenix's little lake. Her eyes wearing a small sparkle Phoenix had never before seen.

Her face, however, was not wearing anything that represented a sparkle, but instead, there was a sort of frown. One of worry,

Phoenix presumed. Or at least something similar.

It was strange. Somehow, at that moment, Phoenix felt like they were the only two people in the room. It was only for a second, but it had seemed like a lifetime. There was just something about looking into those eyes, no matter what sort of expression they were holding. Something that held an aura of mystery, and elegance. Something that held the promise of a secret, a secret of something that is Said Not.

"Miss Hudson, are you all right?"

Phoenix said nothing. Not for a moment, anyway. It was as if she was in shock. She wanted to reply, but she couldn't. Her voice had escaped, run off to join her heart, down in the deepest recesses of her lungs. But it was dark down there, and her words didn't like it.

"I—" They caught in her throat on the way back up. She coughed, and they slid free again. "I'm fine."

Now, if only she could have told her. The truth was no. No, she was not all right. She wasn't coping. She was far weaker than she had first thought. She was living in a small house, cold and dark. No money to pay for heating or electricity. She didn't know how much longer the food would last. She hadn't seen her father in weeks. She didn't know if he were dead or alive. She was lonely and scared. And the daily reminder of where her mother used to be had been staring her in the face, with no distraction, since her father left.

But Phoenix could not say these things; she had to hold it in, as much as it yearned to burst out, she had to control herself. This was not the time. This was not the place. These things she felt, these things were Acceptable Not.

"Are you sure? You look a bit pale."

"Yeah. I'm good," she smiled meekly.

•••

"And that was it. The moment was over, and I was about to be forgotten again." Phoenix choked back the tears that were threatening to escape from her eyes once more. "At the time, I couldn't help but think of myself as stupid, but what was I supposed to do? Tell her everything, right there? In front of everyone? No. These things were better Said Not."

The therapist placed the notebook back on her desk and crossed her legs. "That's very interesting, Phoenix, that you felt that these things were better off not being said. And yet, in the end, she found out anyway."

"Yeah," Phoenix almost laughed as the tears began to roll down her cheeks, "ain't life funny that way?"

The therapist smiled sympathetically.

"But I suppose that was the day I first heard it."

"Heard what?"

"The whisper. The small rasp of breath that seemed to sound something like, *I care*. Perhaps I had heard her wrong, perhaps that whisper was nothing but voices in my head, just like there were voices in my father's. But either way, I idolized her for it. That was it, right then, that's when I fell." Phoenix stopped, picking up a tissue from the box that lay on the table ahead of her and wiping the salty water from her face. "And that was the night of the first dream."

"The first dream?"

The young girl nodded. "I don't know what seemed so special about it. In fact, it was quite ordinary, actually. Nothing special at all. A simple situation, portrayed in a rather boring way, discussing matters of no importance, in a world of what Is Not."

"What happened in the dream?"

"It was basic, normal, uninteresting. I was just sitting there, as I did all the time—you see? Nothing special at all. It may as well have been an average day; it was familiar enough. We were in our usual places. Ms. Davis was behind her walls, and I was behind mine. It was then that she turned from her previous gaze—what that was, I am unsure, but that doesn't matter—and looked at me. Her eyes shone as they always did, sparkling in the late morning light, fixated on my own. I smiled, and she did too. She opened her mouth and spoke. I'm not sure what was Said, in that world of what Is Not. But that didn't matter. But she spoke. As did I. She laughed. So did I. That was it. That was the first."

"Hmm," the therapist took a moment to ponder over what she just heard, rubbing her chin lightly with a forefinger. "It's interesting to hear that the dream, which is something that obviously had a great impact on you, is something that really was of an everyday occurrence."

"I told you it was boring."

"No one said that, Phoenix," the therapist smiled at her. "Let's talk about something else for the moment. Tell me about Christmas."

Phoenix sighed. "It rolled around like it always does. For many other people, this is supposed to be a happy time, when they are away from the busy life of school and work; there's snow to play in, friends to see, and presents to open."

"But not for you?"

Phoenix shook her head. "No, not for me. Not anymore. I missed the not-quite-real world of school. I didn't welcome the cold brought by the harsh blizzards of the winter months, as I sat wrapped in blankets in my unheated home. Juniper was always busy during the vacation. And, of course, there were no presents, either. There had still been no word from my father. However, I managed to get a job during the vacation in a department store. They had needed extra help in the manic Christmas sales, and I needed the money. So, I guess the holidays at least gave me something."

"And what was that?"

"They gave me enough money to get the electricity back up and running," she untangled her finger from its strand and ruffled her hand through her hair. "For a while, anyway."

"What about Christmas day itself?"

Phoenix groaned. "That was definitely something to remember. In a weird sort of way."

"More dreams?"

The young girl nodded. "More everything."

•••

Phoenix had spent her day snacking on pop-tarts and a frozen turkey TV dinner. It wasn't too bad, all considered. Until she ran out of milk, that is. While making her mid-afternoon cup of coffee, Phoenix discovered the carton in the refrigerator to be virtually empty, and she couldn't help but wonder how she'd missed that. Though, in her defense, she had often found her mind was concerned with other things.

She spent a good ten minutes racking her brains for somewhere that was likely to be selling milk on Christmas day, before remembering the small corner store beside the church. They were always open on Christmas day. They were the main supplier for the holiday service next door.

Buying the milk was the easy part. Phoenix still had money from that week's wages, and she somehow managed to make it to the small store before it closed. It was walking back that was the problem.

She had just reached the front gate to the small garden path that led to her front door. Three steps in, and she discovered the delight of when the soles of worn sneakers collide with the slippery surface of frozen water. The milk carton slid from her hand as she slid down to meet the concrete below. Her heart jumped as her body bounced off the ground. Her natural reaction was to use her arms to break the fall. Bad move. She felt the pain shoot up her left wrist as she came coat-to-surface with the substance winter leaves behind. The substance both Juniper and she had met before.

Straightening up again, Phoenix picked up the fallen carton with her right hand, thankful it hadn't split, and headed back inside. After placing the milk in the refrigerator, she sat on the sofa and began to examine her wrist. It wasn't broken, she knew that much. Most likely just sprained. She found some compression bandages in the medicine cabinet. Her father used to use them in his artwork. He used to cut them up and dye them various colors. Or sometimes he'd create shadowy figures, wrapped in scrappy gauze, molded in strange contortions.

But that was Then, and this was Now.

Gauze was no longer used for recreation, but for re-creation. To heal and support. The physical body, that is. For the mental breaks and sprains? Well, the dreams became her gauze for that.

That Christmas night, Phoenix wrapped her body and bandaged wrist into the warmth of her bed and comforter. And her mind escaped, for the second time in those few months.

There she was again, her beautiful face filling Phoenix's mind, and making her feel safe. They were standing in a world of white. Maybe it was reflecting the world outside, or maybe their surroundings just weren't important. Phoenix didn't know. She was simply looking out over the freeing field of light ahead of her, and suddenly, she appeared.

Walking in like an angel to heaven. It was so natural. Her light hair shimmering in the white light, despite the almost hidden secret of her darker horizons; her perfect smile, so understanding, so sincere; her blue eyes shining like an ocean under the summer sun. Phoenix smiled, too, as she came to her, but her eyes only locked with Phoenix's for a second and were soon distracted. From her face they wandered, until they reached her wrist. Phoenix followed her gaze and saw that even here, in this world of dreams, the bandage clasped tightly to her skin. She lifted a delicate arm, and took

Phoenix's hand in hers, examining it closely.

That took Phoenix's breath away. Even in her dream, where anything was possible, it was this act that took her breath away. Her hands, they were so, so... *rough*. It was a surprising contrast to the elegant notions in which she moved them. Her fingernails weren't long and French-tipped as Phoenix had expected—she wasn't sure why she had expected such a thing, it just sort of felt right that she would have nice nails—but instead they were very short, almost non-existent, and ragged. Her fingertips were round, and the skin around them was covered in little scuffs from obvious picking.

But it felt so comfortable. So... *right*.

"You're hurt." Her voice was silvery in the angelic theme of the world that surrounded them. Far softer than the tones Phoenix had ever heard her speak back in that other place, where there were daily lessons, dead mothers, and missing fathers.

Her eyes were crinkled into that sympathetic smile Phoenix loved so much. She felt her touch on her skin and embraced the toughness of this woman's hands, and the warmth they brought to Phoenix's aching joint.

Phoenix nodded, keeping her eyes locked on the other woman's. A smile grew on her face as she scanned Noelle's features once more. No one spoke after that. Phoenix didn't know why. She didn't really care. Just being there, with her, in that wash of white, alone, together, free, comforted. It was magical.

Then, just like before, it ended. The white faded to black, where Phoenix could no longer see the familiar beauty of her face or feel the embrace of her rough touch. And then, she opened her eyes. The view of her room had never come as such a shock. She sat up as fast as she could, pulling back her comforter, and looking down at her wrist. Phoenix unraveled the bindings quickly, for reasons unknown even to herself, as if by taking off the layers she would be able to find the woman's hand still clutching her own beneath. But that was absurd, and Phoenix was faced only with the light purple of her freshly bruising skin.

Taking her other hand, she ran her fingers over the tender area. Closing her eyes, Phoenix thought of the touch as that of another. Caressing the fleshy coverings of her limb with great care. Draining the stiffness away. But no, it wasn't right. Her hands were too cold, too thin, too *soft*.

Phoenix opened her eyes once more, and it hit her. Pain, that's the only word to possibly describe it. Phoenix had thought she was used to pain, but not like this. This hurt more than any blow she'd ever experienced. More than failing an exam, more than her father leaving, and maybe, just maybe, even a little more than the death of her mother.

She didn't like to imagine how that must sound. But with her it was different. They had foreseen the day of her mother's passing. They had been prepared for months, been told by various doctors of her little time left in this world. It was horrible, but at least Phoenix knew. And in knowing, she took some comfort.

But this, this world of what Is Not, and yet what could so easily be—this was a shimmer in the darkness, a light to guide Phoenix through this seemingly endless tunnel, and she'd just awoken to see that it didn't exist. She'd been hit with the reality that her shimmer had been nothing but a trick of the eye; that her guiding light had only been the reflection of a passing car, heading in a different direction, at a hundred miles per hour.

The feeling seemed to explode from her heart and grow across her chest, causing her muscles to tighten in a most uncomfortable fashion; before it moved to her throat, sliding as a lump; and then it hit her face, and the tears fell once more. Though it didn't seem to matter how much she cried, the pain did not leave.

CHAPTER 8

*S*eptember 20*th*

I was married once. Most people don't expect to hear that. I'm not sure why it surprises them so to entertain the idea of a woman such as myself playing the role of the dedicated wife, but the truth was that I adored it; or more correctly, I adored him. *It was Mark's fault, really; he was the one who first introduced us. But he could never have known where it would lead, what wondrous things life would present to us, what horrendous events would eventually take place.*

From the very moment I first laid eyes on him, I knew he was someone I wanted to know. I'm not sure if 'love at first sight' is something I believe in; I have always found that far too cliché to be used in real life. But there was definitely something, something about this staggeringly handsome, tall, dark stranger that left me yearning for more. His irises were these deep brown pits of eternity that I could just fall into, leading me into the mysterious darkness, and I just needed to know what they were hiding.

To this day, I still remember that night so clearly, when we were first to make each other's acquaintance. It was a month after I'd secured my first teaching job at the local state high school, and Mark had called to ask if I'd like to attend a party of one of his professor friends from California. I hadn't been sure of it at first; I was tired, trying to juggle a new job with the odd notion that I was now supposed to be a responsible adult, as opposed to the student mathematician that I'd become so used to being. But he convinced me, as he always did.

•••

"Noelle!" Mark greeted her from the cab when she arrived outside the highfalutin hotel entrance. "Darling, how are you? You look stunning!"

"Oh," she breathed as he embraced her, before looking at his own attire, "and you look... the same as always."

He threw back his head of slowly graying black curls, and laughed loudly, gently ushering her through the grand entrance of the hotel as men in suits and tuxedos flocked around them. That was the thing about Mark; he always was the same. It didn't seem to matter the time or occasion; he looked just as scruffy and, simultaneously, just as brilliant as ever.

It was upon entering the bustling function room that Noelle was at once struck by the incredibly dynamic force that was this crazy man's brilliance. The size of this particular gathering was so much larger than she had thought it would be; the number of distinguished and influential guests that her old professor rubbed shoulders with on a regular basis was far greater than she ever could have imagined. Having evidently noticed the look of awe that had taken over her face, Mark smirked.

"Why the surprise, my dear?"

"When you said a professor from California, I didn't think the majority of Caltech would be in attendance!" She hit him lightly on the shoulder.

"Ha! Well, what can I say? I'm a catch," he smiled at her in that mischievous way he did, the way that caused his eyes to glint with an odd mixture of excitement and something else Noelle hadn't quite been able to name. "Anyway, I have some people for you to meet."

It was then that she took full notice of the circle of people standing right beside them, who she had somehow failed to acknowledge in the whirlwind of this prestigious party. And that was when she first laid eyes on what was to become the most wondrously horrendous part of her soul.

"Noelle Davis," Mark began, pointing his way along the men in the group of intellectuals, "this is Dr. Alistair Charleston, a renowned astronomer—as I'm sure you're aware—he's come all the way from Massachusetts for this party; Professor Bryn Huff, he's from the biochemistry department; Corporal Willard Lewis, from mechanical engineering, who's just come back from—where was it you've been stationed recently, Iraq?"

"Afghanistan," the rather burly gentleman replied, taking a glug of what looked like some kind of ale from a tall glass.

"Right," Mark chuckled, "of course. Willard works in infrastructure in the military; he essentially spends his time building things that other people might bomb, and tries to make sure he doesn't cock it up, isn't that right, Lewis, old boy?"

"Indeed, it is Stevens," this time it was the Corporal who chuckled.

"Never saw the attraction of military service myself," Mark continued, "something about all the fighting that just didn't appeal to me... Anyway, last, but by no means least, this fine young gentleman is Jorge de Melo. Jorge here has been doing an outreach program in some underdeveloped areas, getting the kids all riled up with the basics of science. Absolutely bloody riveting."

Eventually, Mark trailed off, finding himself engaging in more party pleasantry with people from various important positions in the world, and once he had finished with that, he politely excused himself, saying that he 'needed to get going,' and Noelle couldn't help but worry.

It may seem odd that she should worry at such a thing, as it may appear as something that wouldn't cause worry at all, but she still remembered too clearly the first time she had heard Mark use this line before disappearing off into the night. It was by sheer coincidence that on that first night she just so happened to find herself in the same place as he, walking in through a bathroom door she was sure he thought he'd locked. She could still recall the shock on his face when he saw, through the reflection in the mirror in front of him, her figure entering the restroom, her eyes just glancing the last dregs of powder on the counter, the end of the repurposed cocktail straw as he shoved it hastily back into his pocket, and the quick recoil of his hand as he had wiped it across his nose. Noelle had discovered his darkest secret and, somehow, that drew them closer than ever before.

At one point in the evening soon after Mark's hasty exit, Noelle found herself alone with this highly intriguing Mr. de Melo.

"So, Jorge, where are you from originally?" she inquired, taking the first step to talk to this perfect stranger, feeling giddy as a teenage girl as she tried to stop her voice from revealing the nervous flutter that was rising in her stomach. It was ridiculous, really. She couldn't think of any other situation in her life that had made her feel quite so much like she was an awkward fourteen-year-old again, trying to make the cool kids like her.

"Brazil," he smiled, and Noelle could swear her heart almost melted, "but I live all over the place these days."

"How so?"

"Work," he took a sip of the martini held between his large fingers. He'd had such a firm handshake.

"What sort of work?" She couldn't help but find herself biting lightly at the corner of her lips and feeling incredibly foolish for it at the same time.

"With children, mainly," he continued, the movements of his mouth strangely enchanting, "I tend to go around some of the less established villages and help with things like basic literacy and numeracy skills with the younger ones, and English and science with those who are slightly older. What about you? How do you spend your time?"

"Oh," she felt the blush rise in her cheeks, "I actually work with kids, too; I'm a Math teacher in a high school."

"Really?" Noelle watched as his face sparked with what seemed like a genuine interest. "Wow, how do you find that?"

"You know, I actually love it. I really wasn't sure at first, about the whole teaching thing, I mean. It wasn't really even my idea, more something that my mother got me looking at. But the more I got into it, I found that I had this unique opportunity to teach what it was that helped kids grow. I mean, I know I'm only a Math teacher, but I feel like I get to contribute to the molding of these kids, and see their personalities as they develop. I get to be a part of the experiences that guide them into the real world, and to the knowledge that might aid them throughout the years to come. It's like I get to play a small part in the life of each and every student that walks through my classroom door." She trailed off, and gently put her hand in front of her mouth, the blush that had never entirely left coming back fully to her cheeks. "Oh gosh, I hope that doesn't sound super lame."

He smiled back at her. "Not at all."

•••

That was the first conversation we ever had. Even to this day I lack the ability to fully explain, or even comprehend, what it was that made us such a perfect match—we just were. Four years later, and we were married. Mr. and Mrs. de Melo. What I had with him was the kind of love that poets write about, the kind of love that I thought only existed in fairytales and movies. He truly was my other half, completing my soul against the mighty wrath of Zeus, bringing us together as a whole once more. And for a moment, I almost started to believe that dreams really could come true. Almost.

Noelle stopped and put the pen down. She really didn't like this whole journaling thing; she found it difficult to see any benefits from it. All it seemed to do was bring up things from her past; things that she wished would just stay there.

But, then again, maybe it was healthy to write it all down, to go through everything in her life and make sense of all the things she had lived through; all that things that shaped where, and who, she was today.

And there it was again—the day Noelle had learned what it was to truly be alone, pushing its way into her mind once more.

The world fell apart on a Friday. Jorge and I had been living in Brazil together for a few years by that point; he'd been continuing his work with outreach kids, and I'd been employed as a teacher in the local high school. And for the first time in what seemed like my whole life, I was really, truly, undeniably happy. But, of course, it couldn't last. Nothing perfect lasts forever, but god, wouldn't that be nice?

As much as I wish it wasn't so, I remember this day so clearly; every miniature detail hangs in my mind fully formed in four dimensions.

There had been a parent-teacher evening at the school, and I'd been stuck there all evening, talking in-depth about all the children and their varying degrees of ability in the field of mathematics. I often wonder that had I been at home earlier that day, had I been able to observe the mannerisms of my husband, would I have perhaps noticed something, anything *out of the ordinary? Would I have noted a difference in his demeanor? A change in his attitude? Anything that could have hinted at what was to come? Anything that could have saved him? They all tell me 'no.' No, there was nothing I could do. But I guess I'll never know.*

She had only been home fifteen minutes when it happened. Jorge had greeted her in the living room as she had entered the house, kissing her as she placed her bag on the sofa, and as she then headed upstairs to change, he walked into the kitchen to make them dinner.

Noelle had just pulled a gray cashmere sweater over her head when she heard it, the sound of glass shattering from below. For a moment she just stood, listening for signs of anything else, but was met with only silence.

"Honey?" she called as she hopped down the stairs. No reply.

It was his legs that Noelle saw first. She could still recall how the laces of his shoes danced along the tiled floor as his muscles jerked violently, the way they twisted and twirled across the ceramic stage. Rushing over to him, she ignored her heart as it threatened to jump out of her mouth, and fell to the ground beside his convulsing form, not even stopping to take notice of the broken wine glass she was kneeling upon, not feeling the shards as they dug into her knees. She was unable to stop herself from hyperventilating as hot tears fell down her cheeks at the sight of the thick, scarlet rivers of life that were running from the face of the man she loved the most. His usually deep chocolate irises were blank and stained by the ruptured vessels in his eyes, his large nostrils like open floodgates as the blood poured from them, joining with the streams that trickled from his ears to create an ocean of red sea on their kitchen floor.

Subarachnoid hemorrhage, they said. Caused by an aneurysm, they said. Nothing I could have done, they said. But I didn't care what they said; no one could bring my husband back to me. No one could fill the emptiness that had come when the other half of my soul had been ripped away from me. The gods were cruel, and it would seem that Zeus would have his way after all.

CHAPTER 9

Phoenix followed the second hand of the clock with her eyes as it ticked on by, counting the rhythmic beat that syncopated with the beat of her own heart. It was odd to be alone in the office, with no one asking her a million questions about her life. She felt almost like she had when she'd entered that room for the first time, taking note once more of the marks on the floor, the color of the walls, as if they were old acquaintances that she hadn't seen in a while. She'd been too busy stuck in the Then to take notice of the Now for some time. A part of her almost wanted to apologize to her surroundings, to say sorry for not paying attention; for ignoring them while she was stuck in her own head.

Then she heard the swing of the door behind her, and she moved the room to the back of her mind.

"Okay," the therapist breathed as she closed the door and took a seat opposite Phoenix, putting the two of them back in their usual places. "Sorry, I'm late."

"That's fine."

"So," the therapist began, quickly moving on from the topic of the surrounding room, to which only Phoenix had been privy, "last session we spoke about Christmas, and all the troubles you encountered over that time. And the beginning of the dreams, of course."

"Right," Phoenix nodded.

"So, what happened after that?"

The young girl sighed. "School commenced about a week later. When I met up with Juniper again, she was full of stories of the vacation. She had seen that boy a lot over the weeks we'd been on break, and she was explaining every detail about their midnight adventures. It was a difficult conversation to listen to."

"And why was it difficult?"

She shrugged. "I don't know. It wasn't that I didn't want to listen to her, but she was speaking about a boy I'd never met, about activities I'd never heard of, and arguments with which I did not agree."

The woman frowned. "Arguments?"

"Yeah," Phoenix rolled her eyes, "from the sound of things, they argued a lot. I don't think that was good for Juniper. She seemed to put it down to the fact that they both had strong personalities, but I wondered if he was taking advantage of her. Insulting her very being, and then getting let off for it by defending his case as being a—" she raised her fingers to signify inverted commas, *"fiery individual, who was in love with another.* I mean, who the hell says stuff like that? Anyway, as much as I tried to listen to Juniper's complaints about Christmas, I was distracted. It didn't take much; all she did was walk past."

"Noelle?"

Phoenix nodded. "Yeah, and it was like I was locked in again."

The therapist thought about this for a moment. "Locked in?"

"Yeah, I was seeing her in person, for the first time since the dream, and I couldn't help but slip my hand over my wrist as she drifted by," Phoenix also couldn't help herself from unconsciously doing the same again as she recalled the event, her fingers lightly gliding over her opposite hand, forming little circles upon her sleeve. "I even turned my head as she continued walking, and I felt that pain again, the same pain I felt after I'd woken up. But all I could do was hold it in. After all, I couldn't just start crying where I was, in the middle of the school corridor, where all was so exposed. It just couldn't happen.

"Then, in the blink of an eye, she was out of sight, and my attention turned back to Juniper," the girl sighed, moving both of her hands apart to rest them on the arms of the chair in which she was seated. "I remember her smiling at the excitement of her new partner, and I smiled back, no matter how much I felt like crying at that moment. Juniper then lifted her arm and showed me the bracelet he'd gotten her for Christmas. Though then added that she'd thrown it back at him in a fight, but they made up, so she put it back on."

"It certainly does sound like they argued a lot."

Phoenix sat upright in her chair. "It's that word—*love*. It does things to people, crazy things. And that's just when love happens to be Acceptable. They never tell you what happens when the love is Acceptable Not..." She paused. "It is surprisingly easy to destroy the ones you love, and even easier to be destroyed by them."

The therapist pushed her glasses back up to the top of her nose. "What makes you say that?"

"Because of what happened next."

"And what happened next, Phoenix?"

Phoenix looked at the woman, her hazel irises locking upon the lenses of the glasses across from her, her icy gaze almost enough to send a chill throughout the room. "The start of it all," she said flatly, "the beginning of the end."

•••

The harsh beauty of winter passed, and the warmth of spring sprung into their lives once more. Phoenix's wrist had pretty much healed by then, though she still found trouble with certain actions.

It was during the lunch break of a warm spring morning that the events took place. *Those* events; the type that come bursting into one's world, changing life as they know it forever.

The weather was wonderful; the sky was clear, the temperature high, and although the ground still sparkled with the rainfall of the previous night, there was not a cloud in sight. Phoenix couldn't rightly remember where it was that she was heading that day—just wandering the grounds, perhaps; breathing in the fresh new air—but whatever her intention, she was soon distracted.

It was as Phoenix passed the large gates that led to the running track that she heard the voices. They were harsh, fast, angry. And coming from beneath the bleachers. She didn't know what had taken hold of her that morning, but curiosity reigned, and she followed the sound of irritated human conversation. As she got closer, she began to decipher the people. It was a girl and a boy. The girl, she recognized almost at once. It was so familiar, so haunting, so fast, so... *Juniper.*

Phoenix could see through the lines of the bleachers now. She was right; it *was* Juniper. And the male voice, well, that was her boyfriend. They were standing opposite each other, yelling, pointing, grabbing hair, and jabbing chests. It was difficult to see a clear picture through the sliced world of light that the rows of benches offered her, but Phoenix could see enough, and she could hear perfectly.

She watched from her hidden position through the railings as he stumbled toward the girl. He seemed uneasy on his feet, and for a moment, Phoenix wondered if she had hit him. But then she saw the bottle in his hand. She had often forgotten that he was one of *those* kids, the ones who snuck bottles of vodka into school and hid them under benches and above plasterboard ceiling tiles. Phoenix tried to follow what was happening through the gaps in the rails, but she kept losing long, horizontal slices of action.

The high shriek came from Juniper as the tinkling sound of broken glass shattered through the air. He must have thrown it above her, as Phoenix doubted it would have had that reaction had it hit the frail female form. This time it was Juniper who struck out. As Phoenix watched her pull her palm back, she assumed she was going to slap him, but the sound of impact never came. Instead, Phoenix watched as in one swift movement she swiped her hand in front of his face. At first, Phoenix thought she'd missed, but then she heard his own, deeper cry, and saw the droplets of blood beading on his skin. She'd scratched him.

What happened next was something Phoenix had never expected, and she often wondered that had she decided to make her presence known, and perhaps tried to interfere in the fight sooner, then maybe the outcome would have been quite different. Juniper was a feisty girl, but guts alone didn't give you a physical advantage over an athletic male with anger issues. Before Phoenix knew what was happening, he was on top of her, pinning her to the ground below. Holding her wrists tightly against the gravel, grinding them further into the dust every time she tried to wriggle free. Phoenix couldn't help but brush her own wrist as she watched the scene play out.

He bent down further toward her face, and Phoenix had to strain her ears to hear what he was saying. But as she pressed her head against the slit in the metal, she caught the words that cut Juniper's spirit.

"Worthless little bitch, no better than your junkie whore of a mother."

That was it. Phoenix couldn't stay hidden any longer. So, she jumped out from behind her hidden pillar, and into the heart of the fire.

"Hey!" she yelled as she approached them. "What the hell are you doing? Get away from her!"

Phoenix couldn't have sounded very threatening, but it seemed to do the trick. She presumed he was more surprised at being caught off guard than his reaction having anything to do with either her presence or the words that came tumbling out of her mouth. She didn't care. He stood up and staggered away. She waited until he was out of sight, and ran over to Juniper, who lay crying beneath the metal skeleton of the empty bleachers.

"God, Juniper, what the hell have I missed?"

"It's like I've let him back me into a corner," she began, weeping, "and instead of fighting my way out of it, I let him get to me. He's won."

Phoenix tried her best to comfort her friend. She helped her first to sit, and handed her two tissues from her pocket; one for her tears, and one for the blood she had noticed dripping from her nose. Once she had calmed down somewhat, Phoenix attempted to discuss what they should do.

"What do you mean?" Juniper sobbed, wiping black lines from beneath her eyes.

"Well, we have to tell someone. He was drunk, and he *assaulted* you!" Phoenix ran a hand through her hair, trying also to calm her own nerves at the situation. "We've got to tell a teacher, maybe the police—"

"No!" Her reaction was instant. "No, we can't do that."

"But, Juniper—"

"I said no, Phoenix." Her mind was made up. There was no reasoning with her. Not then, not ever.

•••

The therapist frowned lightly. "That doesn't sound like a good situation, Phoenix. It must've been hard for you to see that."

Phoenix almost laughed. "Hard for me to see that? Are you serious? The person that was hard for was Juniper." She then

106

suddenly turned somber. "And I just wish I'd known how hard it really was for her at the time."

"And why is that?

"Because it wasn't long after the day under the bleachers that it happened."

"Oh..." the therapist paused for a moment and rearranged her seating position. "Are you able to talk about that?"

Phoenix took a deep breath and nodded slowly. She'd told this woman about almost everything else, so why not this?

"It was only two weeks later that her household went out for the day. They went out to a theme park, and even though they'd asked Juniper to come, she declined the offer. I don't think that they thought much of it at the time. I mean, we're teenage girls—they probably thought that she had homework to do, or music to listen to, or friends to invite places. So, they just let it be. But little did they know that she already had plans. Plans, which were very much Said Not. Juniper didn't know that I was going to come over. I didn't even know that I was going to come over; it was just a Decision that I'd made on a whim."

"What do you think made you want to go over there?"

The young girl shrugged. "I'd awoken that morning feeling the same as I had on many others since my dad left. I was lonely. My night had been full of dreams of Noelle again, and waking to the emptiness of my house had been just a little too much for me that day. So, I got dressed and decided that I'd go and visit Juniper. See how she was doing since… well, since the happening of the incident that had remained very much Said Not."

•••

Phoenix had walked up to the front door of Juniper's house and knocked once, to let her know she was there, before walking in. This had always been the way in the few times she had been to Juniper's home. In the Golding house, knocking was seen as an introduction, not a question of entering. There was little time to spare running around letting people in through doors when they were perfectly capable of doing such on their own. She began calling Juniper's name as she stepped into the hallway, closing the door behind her. To her surprise, there was no answer. The house stood in a perfect silence, the only light noise coming from the clock on the mantelpiece.

The floorboards creaked beneath Phoenix's feet as she wandered farther into the seemingly deserted house. She was confused. Surely the door would only be left unlocked if there were at least *someone* in the house. She knew the Goldings were open, but no one was *that* open, surely. She continued through the house, sticking her head briefly into the lounge, just to check if Juniper had fallen asleep on the couch or something, but she wasn't there.

After she had cleared the ground floor and still found no trace of her, Phoenix went upstairs and approached her room. As she did so, she could see that Juniper's door was slightly ajar. So, she called her name—and still, no reply. She continued toward the door, her feet still causing the floor beneath her to creak unnervingly. She placed her hands against the cool of the lightwood, and slowly pushed it open.

Phoenix gasped at the sight behind the door. She had found Juniper. Her bare feet dangling in elegance, toes pointed like a floating ballerina. The black skirt that had been placed against her skull leggings flared lightly as it twisted slowly. Her long, dyed midnight blue locks covered her ivory face completely, flowing gently over her shoulders.

Yes, Phoenix had found Juniper. Found her hanging.

For a painfully long minute, she just stood there. Staring. Not breathing. Not thinking. Just staring.

Then the minute came to an end, and without really thinking about what she was doing, she grabbed the small stool lying beside her bed and clambered onto it.

Reaching her hands into the noose, Phoenix slipped her fingers between the rope and Juniper's bluing skin, not even feeling the burning of her fingers as they scraped against the course material, tearing away the outer layers of her skin as she wrestled against it. And with all her might she loosened it enough to pull it over the girl's head. She extended an arm as her body fell to the ground, yet all that did was pull Phoenix down with her.

They landed in a heap atop the rough carpet. Juniper's cold frame lying limp across her own. Phoenix rolled the girl off her torso, and onto her back. Calling her name over and over, her own heart fluttering violently in her chest as she did so. Tears welling in her eyes and beginning to fall lightly as she pleaded with the silent figure.

But everything was blue—her hair, her eyes, her lips.

Phoenix pulled out her cell and dialed for an ambulance. The emergency services came, and she stood in the downstairs hallway, watching through a blurred screen as the two paramedics rolled her friend out on a stretcher. They didn't seem to be in any hurry. But who was she to say? It would seem that Phoenix had lost her sense of time entirely. And her sense of sound. The world felt silent and slow. The people moving past her like those from a movie. The only sounds being the deep thump of the heart that occupied her own chest, and the monotone ticking of the clock on the mantelpiece.

The ambulance pulled away slowly. No siren was used.

CHAPTER 10

October 5th

Empedocles established that there are four ultimate elements that make up all the structures in the world and that the difference of each structure was produced by the proportions in which these elements were combined. He believed that these elements were changed by them being brought together and then taken apart by two divine powers—Love and Strife. Can you just imagine it? The pull of an attraction so strong that the poor element has no way of escaping its fate of being joined together with another? And then, just as it settles into something new, being ripped apart, changed utterly? And to have this process repeated over, and over, and over again, into eternity?

But that's the thing with these sovereign masters of Love and Strife; they work in perfect harmony.

Do not misunderstand me; I am not naïve. But sometimes, the world really is exactly as you see it. And sometimes, it's not. Galileo declared that 'the language of Nature is mathematics' and for the longest time, I wholeheartedly agreed. But as I grew older, as I experienced more of what it means to be human, to love and have lost, my faith began to crumble. Maybe this is where my fascination with numbers originated, not from a pure interest in empirical knowledge at all, but from some deep-seated need to understand nature and the

111

reasons why things played out the way they did. Why once heroic fathers brought home foreign wives, why husbands sailed off in rivers of blood, and why best friends faded away…

I know what it's like to lose a best friend, to find yourself all alone in the world, feeling your way through the dark like an infant trying to find its feet. After the death of my husband, I no longer had any need to stay in Brazil, so I left for home, and that was how I found myself living in Mark's spare room. I can still barely believe how lucky I was to have a friend like my old professor in my life, especially then, when I found myself with almost nowhere else to turn. My father and his third wife were living in a one-bedroomed villa at the time, and, as much as I love her, I would have done almost anything to keep from moving back in with my mother. My brother had just married his childhood sweetheart, and the arrival of my nephew on Kirsten's side meant that it would have been a great inconvenience to either sibling to be landed with housing their freshly widowed sister.

Yes, the arrival of my nephew. Simultaneously the best and worst thing to enter my life since Brazil. Born weighing 7lbs 4oz, he was the most beautiful thing I'd ever seen on this planet, making me the proudest aunt in the world. It was just the way his big blue eyes looked around him at the everyday extraordinary items that filled the surrounding space; the way his tiny hand could grip so firmly around only one of my own fingers; and the way he looked at you with pure puzzlement whenever he had the hiccups that made me love him more than I could ever imagine loving anything instantaneously.

Well, maybe not anything. As harsh as it may sound, I can certainly imagine one thing I may have loved more. And that one thing would have been a child of my own.

Noelle sighed. That wasn't an option for her. She had since resigned herself to the fact that she was never going to be a mother. It wasn't that she was too old; she knew plenty of people who'd had kids from their late 30s into their early 40s. But the reason instead that kept her from it was that she was too broken. She could barely carry the weight of being herself in this world, and it wasn't fair to bring a baby into the whirlwind that was her life.

No, having a baby isn't an option anymore. How could I possibly have a child when I'm missing half of my soul?

She put the pen down for a minute and rubbed her temples. Who knew journaling would be this hard? Taking a deep breath, she looked back at the paper ahead of her and tried to continue.

Mark had always had a way of making things seem bearable for me, even if he couldn't do the same for himself. He had started the partying lifestyle in his younger years, and as he grew older, the mindset never really left. It all started back in high school with his first serious boyfriend. This boy—whose name I never knew—had been one of the more artistic and free souls in his life. He'd spent his time bunking off school, smoking dope, and creating these wonderfully psychedelic masterpieces around town in a very Banksy-esque sort of way. He was the driving force behind Mark's own creative freedom for a long time, as he found a way to mix his world of physics and numbers with this boy's paints and colors. But creativity wasn't the only thing Mark got into.

I was never sure what age he was exactly when he started on the class As, but by the time I met him, this doomed romance was already well underway. Of course, I didn't realize it back then. I didn't realize it at all until that night I saw him in the bathroom at that party. He changed after that. It seemed to bring us closer, and he no longer hid any of it from me ever again. I often think back to this and wonder why, why did he just decide that due to some twist of fate that amounted to me seeing what I saw meant that he acted the way he did? Why didn't he just pretend it never happened? Or why didn't he try to convince me that it wasn't what I thought it was? Well, honestly, I think he was relieved. He was living his life with this invisible burden on his shoulders, and for the first time in a long time, he didn't have to pretend to be someone he wasn't anymore.

So, maybe I should have seen it coming. They all talk about 'the needle and the damage done' but no-one really listens to Neil Young until it's too late.

And there she was, making her home in the spare room of a rundown old apartment with brown-patched curtains on the windows that fell just short of the floor. It may have seemed a wonder how a man such as Physics Professor Mark Stevens lived in such a detestable hovel. But the answer is quite simple, really—as undeniably brilliant as Mark was, he was also undeniably and infinitely short of cash.

Noelle supposed he must have had money once—after all, with his experience and qualifications he should have been getting paid for every mathematical sentence that came out of his mouth. But by the time she moved in with him, he'd been unemployed for three years. That was the thing about working as a university lecturer; you could only keep your job if you were sober enough to actually lecture.

Noelle remembered sitting with him on the couch one day. The worn material of the sofa was warm beneath her bare feet as she sat curled up in a blanket, his arms around her, a bottle of wine between them, and an empty one lying on the wooden planks below. This wasn't an uncommon occurrence in that year they lived as housemates. She was still—and to some extent always would be—very much in mourning from all that had taken place since the abrupt end to her marriage, and as much as she was later to realize that this was the wrong thing to do, kept trying to push herself to move on.

"My brother is married, my sister has a beautiful baby boy, and here I am surrounded by the remnants of what I used to be," she sobbed into the blanket, her whole being seeming little more than a well of self-pity and alcohol. "Why is it, Mark, that I've watched the world heal into something whole after witnessing its utter destruction, and I still can't find it in me to just be happy?"

"The world can heal as much as it likes, my dear," he explained softly, "but the scars will always remind you of that which you wish to forget."

I was at a job interview when I got the call. I can still remember sitting in the principal's office as the buzzing erupted in my pocket, I remember being embarrassed for the distraction, I remember turning off my phone. It wasn't for another forty minutes, once I'd left the interview, and was standing outside waiting for a cab that I bothered to check the voicemail. And suddenly, the world stopped spinning.

The first thing I did was jump into a cab heading to the hospital. I ran through the automatic doors of the ER, and up to the reception desk... and then it all becomes a bit of a blur. I'm not sure who it was that told me, or what it was that they said exactly. But the bottom line was that I was too late, he was gone.

One minute he was there, and then he wasn't. Such was the fleeting nature of the late and great Professor Mark Stevens.

•••

"Noelle." She looked up from the comfortable stare she appeared to have adopted in the middle of the staffroom floor. "Are you all right?"

"Sorry?" She blinked, trying to bring herself back to the present. Fraser stood over her; his large frame suddenly very visible in the afternoon light.

"Are you okay?"

"Oh, yes," she shook the memories from her head. "Sorry, what did you say?"

"The funeral, for the Chambers girl, are you going?"

"Oh, yes, of course," she breathed, still trying, as many of her colleagues were, to fully come to terms with the news of this young student's recent passing. She couldn't help but feel a familiar pang within her own soul when she'd first heard—the familiar pang that often came with untimely death, the one that is fundamentally just an odd concoction of loss and empathy all mixed into one.

The day of the funeral came about quickly, and a surprisingly large number of people cropped up for the occasion. Noelle would have loved to say they were all there to pay their respects to the poor girl, to offer sympathy to those who had lost, to atone for the wrongs they had done to her, but she feared that wasn't the case. She feared it was far more likely that they were there simply in attendance to be a part of the crowd, to try and catch any juicy details of the tragedy. It was the current talk of the school, after all. And by the next week, Noelle was sure they'd have moved on to something else, something new, and will have forgotten this unfortunate girl by the name of Juniper Chambers as she lay rotting in the ground below.

But Noelle wouldn't forget. She may not have known the girl, she may not have known her story, but she understood her struggle. And in solidarity, she poured all of her empathy into a single rose, and placed it upon her coffin, in the hopes that somehow, somewhere in the afterlife—or wherever one goes when they cease to walk this Earth—she would feel the similarity in suffering, and would not be so alone.

CHAPTER 11

"People often ask me why I play the violin," Phoenix mused, playing with her usual strand of her hair, pulling it down through her fingers, feeling the cold smoothness of the flattened tresses as they passed over her skin.

"Really?" The therapist smiled her smile. Phoenix was so used to it now that she didn't even think about it when the corners of the woman's lips curled, no longer bothered to analyze what it might mean, no longer cared.

"Well, in saying that people often ask me, what I really mean is that strangers I don't really know have a tendency to ask whenever they happen to see me carrying it. But my answer is always the same."

"And what answer is that?"

Phoenix looked up from her hair and smiled back. "Because it's ethereal."

"How so?"

"The strings, they seem to hold hundreds of little secrets. Secrets that can only be unveiled when the yielded bow escapes from the player's control and takes on a life of its own…

"And when the melodies burst from their minute cylindrical prisons, they create an invisible artwork. An audible world of everything that Is and Is Not, writing tales of great sorrow and eternal love; explaining history's lessons in pure—though, in my case, *alternative*—classical beauty. That is why I play the violin."

The therapist turned and took a file from her desk, pushing her glasses back toward the bridge of her nose, and flicked through a few pages. "It says here that you were asked to play at Juniper's funeral."

Phoenix froze. Even her breath caught in her throat. "Yes," she choked out quietly.

"And did you?"

"No."

The therapist put the file to one side. "Why not?"

The young girl put her head in her hands, and whispered, "I just couldn't."

•••

It was four days after Juniper's suicide that Phoenix received the note. She knew that it was from her the moment she'd picked it out of her mailbox. Her first reaction was one of great confusion, but that had quickly passed once she'd spied the date in the corner of the envelope. And at that moment Phoenix understood. She'd planned it all out, and this was Juniper's explanation to her. Her way of making things Said.

Phoenix took the message from beyond the grave into the living room and read it while sitting on her sofa:

> Phoenix,
>
> I need you to know that you have always been my best friend. You have saved me from myself more than you know, and I'm so sorry that it's been in vain. You have to understand, there was nothing you could do to stop this. Please, never blame yourself.
>
> Before, it was like being surrounded by dark clouds, and all I could see was myself and the blackness that engulfed me. Now, it feels like I'm in a glass box. I can see everything perfectly clearly, but I'll never be a part of it. I've come to accept that now.
>
> I find that my chest always feels heavy. It's the feeling of intense loss all over again. You think you can move on, and it just comes back. The grief, the memories, the voices in your head that taunt you endlessly.
>
> I just couldn't take it anymore. I'm sorry. I only hope that one day you might find it in your heart to forgive me. Don't let your heart be the same as mine. Don't hold on to what is lost. Let me go.

Love always,

Juniper

Yes, at that moment, Phoenix understood. Her hand fell limply to her side, letting the paper drift to the wooden floor below. So, there she was, the ringing of the silent house around her reaching an unbearable pitch as it rang through her ears, into her brain, swirling 'round and 'round and 'round.

Her eyes were wide; all she could do was stare. She sat on her sofa, staring at the wall ahead of her, not knowing what else to do—unable to move, her limbs stuck by her sides, her legs too weak for her to stand. She just sat, and she stared. All of what was Said Not had finally been Said.

Her thoughts were blank, she wasn't even thinking about Juniper; she wasn't thinking at all. She didn't have any opinion on the world around her, on the funeral that was to come, on the breeze tugging at her clothes through the open window as she sat. She had nothing to say. It would seem that she had become both physically and mentally speechless.

Phoenix stayed this way for what seemed like hours, not hearing any other noise in the small cottage she called home, not hearing anything, anything at all. Anything except the sound of the high-pitched ringing in her ears. And then, all at once, it ended. The overwhelming feeling of numbness that had held her motionless for so long slowly started to break apart.

•••

"That sounds awful, Phoenix," the therapist said gently, her brows furrowed slightly.

"It was," she replied blankly. "So, no, I didn't play the violin at the funeral. I could barely do anything," she sighed. "I've always hated funerals. I'm not sure why, but it's most likely due to the usual reasons people hate funerals, I guess. But this funeral, this was *Juniper's* funeral, and it was worse than any other could possibly be. Ever. My mother had never had a funeral. But Juniper did."

"That must have been really difficult for you."

Phoenix began chewing at the corner of her lips as she looked back up at the woman sitting opposite her.

"But Juniper would have no cares in that world of black, just dreams, right?" The therapist gestured her hands gently to indicate that she didn't know. "I like dreams; they're the only time I can fly to where I want to be. I love that feeling, the one where you slip into that world of paradise, where all is fine, and you get to feel happy. You know, before you come crashing back into reality, and the tears soak your face once more."

"Did you cry at the funeral, Phoenix?"

She shook her head. "No. It was too strange for me to cry. Too surreal. But I remember it clearly. Like a nightmare that lingers in your mind for too long after waking."

●●●

The moisture in the air was settling comfortably upon the tips of the thin blades of grass, the gloss of the mahogany coffin gathering its own beads of water. Mist blinded Phoenix's vision at every corner, clouding out the rest of the world, leaving the coffin in front of her as the only scene in her head.

A single rose lay still upon its shining surface, and Phoenix couldn't help but let a small smile twitch at the corner of her lips. Roses. Whoever had placed such a flower in this place deserved a great gesture.

Phoenix looked around at the crowd of people circled around the central coffin, a welcomed distraction to the inescapable fact that was staring her in the face.

Yes, she looked at the others standing around, and as she looked at each individual face, she couldn't help but wonder why they were there.

They'd never cared when Juniper was alive, but now she was gone, they were all suddenly her best friends. But that wasn't true. Phoenix was her best friend. Phoenix was her *only* friend, and Juniper had been hers. And now, it would seem, she had no one.

The faces were familiar—most, at least. Her foster parents were there, standing across from Phoenix; Mr. Golding supported his wife, as she cried into a cloth handkerchief. There had been some small whisperings since the news of her death. It would seem that people were criticizing them for leaving her behind, that they took her under their roof and should have been there to support her well-being. But it wasn't their fault, Phoenix knew that, and putting any of this on them wasn't fair.

A few others from their school were there. Phoenix wasn't sure why. No one really knew her. Not like she did. Not at all.

Ash—the boy she'd been dating; the boy who, in Phoenix's opinion, had probably killed her—stood to her right, his dark suit looking inappropriately fetching in the last dregs of morning light. It disgusted her. She despised him. Ever since that day under the bleachers, everything about him grated with her. It was enough to turn any look bitter, to feel that urge of utter repulsion whenever he happened to fall into her line of vision. And there he was, right next to her, standing over the body of her dearest friend. He had picked up the little berry, already fallen from her shrub, and squashed it between his fingers.

There was, however, another woman there. Someone she recognized. Someone she searched for in a crowd. Someone she saw in her dreams. Someone she *loved*.

Phoenix didn't know why she was there. Following in with the crowd of other teachers and the principal, she supposed. But she was happy to see her, even if she didn't seem to notice her in return. The strangest people to grace her presence that day were indeed the burial workers who, for some reason, had decided to show up early to view the ceremony. Phoenix never did understand why such impersonal beings were suddenly in this place of solemn love. It was a funeral, and she was distraught, as she had been since the time she'd first laid eyes on Juniper that fateful day. And this was their turn to say goodbye, to make up all the love for the time that was stolen from them. But it would seem that they were not alone, and she didn't get that chance.

The main part of the day came to a close, and they were all ushered into various cabs and cars that led to the wake. That was always a concept that Phoenix found strange; why funerals had an after party, she'd never know. But on this occasion, she was glad they did.

It was in the small room that they had all been crammed into that she spotted her once more. Ms. Davis. She looked extraordinary. Her long dress sliding down her short body like licks of charcoal; her golden locks held in a tidy bun atop her head; her rough fingers picking anxiously at her thumbs.

And it was then, at that moment, that Phoenix realized what Juniper had taught her. Life was short. That was the fact of what Is. When something as extraordinary as an angel with rough hands enters your life, you have to do something about it. And she wasn't about to let her walk out again. Whether it was Acceptable, or —as it was in this case—Acceptable Not.

But not there. Not Then. So, what was Said Not remained.

•••

"Is that strange?" Phoenix looked up at her therapist with a face of mixed emotion. "That during my best friend's funeral, I was wondering about Noelle?"

The woman sighed. "I don't think it's strange, Phoenix. It was a very difficult and emotional time for you, and you didn't have anyone else at the time to help you through that, so it's natural that you'd look up to someone you admire."

Phoenix nodded slowly, letting the words work their way into her brain, allowing them to give her a sense of validation in her feelings. "I saw her around a lot after that."

"Noelle?"

"Yeah," she breathed, as the silent tears began to fall freely down her face, "but I guess that wasn't surprising. She was still the same; it was me who had changed. Every time I saw her, my love grew a little more. I watched her when she was around and found her true self, the one that was hidden beneath the person she showed to people. I mean, she was that person as well—the loud, confident woman. Most definitely. But there was another side to her, the one that had let go of that whisper, and she wasn't as rare as you might think. The more I watched, the more I saw, the more I loved.

"And my dreams, my fabulous dreams, they didn't stop. In fact, they just got better. They had grown longer, and more detailed, and I loved every moment of them. It made me look forward to sleep even more than before. But from every dream, you must awake, and when I did, things were much worse. That was the price, you see, the dreams would be the perfect paradise, and in return, the world around me seemed only to get worse. So, I took a step. A step that seemed to set a ball rolling. A step that was sorely yearned, and yet one that had I not taken may have saved a world of trouble."

•••

It was in the third week of May that she finally plucked up the courage. Phoenix had spotted Noelle walking down a path that led through the center of the school grounds, and started toward her, repeating her intent over and over in her head, in some hopes that it might calm her nerves enough as not to make a blundering fool of herself. That was truly the last thing she needed.

"Ms. Davis," she called as she came up beside her. She looked at her, seemingly confused at first, but then shook her head and smiled. Not a normal smile, but the smile that was unmistakably unique to her—plump cheeks and little lines around her eyes—the smile that haunted her dreams.

"Miss Hudson."

"May I have a moment to speak with you?"

She smiled her smile once more. "Walk with me."

They walked through the cool of the new May air, the daffodils hanging melancholily at the side of the road, their heads drooping and swaying lightly in the breeze of the late morning gloam. They walked undisturbed. The only sound about them being the rustle of the late blooms and the infrequent low rumblings of traffic in the distance.

"So," she said, breaking the silence between them, "what did you want to speak with me about?"

Phoenix's mouth opened, but no sound came out. She couldn't believe it. Not here, not Now. All the words were in her head, practiced over and over again, and yet none would come.

Her heart caught in her throat, butterflies exploding in her gut as she began to stutter nothing but vowels. She stopped, clenching her jaw, and swallowing the letters that never formed into words.

Ms. Davis smiled sympathetically as Phoenix looked at her feet. Phoenix didn't know why she did that. Perhaps she wanted her to know what she was feeling; after all, she was still the one Phoenix found a strange comfort in. Even if she had no idea. Maybe, just maybe, Phoenix was asking for help. She knew it didn't seem like much, but to her—and to this woman as well, perhaps—it was the small things that made all the difference, the small things that held any real meaning.

The dramas were the things everyone noticed; the large shows that supposedly yelled the inside out, the extravagant performances that expressed the burst of built up pain, and the bawdiness of the self-appointed free spirits. Turning people's heads as they walked, catching their attention and holding it hostage, refusing to release it to the greater causes. But for them, that was not the case.

It was the small things, the quiet things; the whispers that, when amplified, proved to be much more than insane ramblings. The twitches of nervous minds, leaving a small open gap for the deepest and darkest of lost souls to peer out into the world. A minuscule gesture that could intend the loudest cry for help to ever be heard.

And so, Phoenix instantly regretted it. The flicker of eyes to feet as opposed to the usual gaze of wandering minds, connected by the strength of shared optics, was enough. Such an insignificant thing, which sent instant warning signals down her spine.

Yet somehow, Phoenix sensed that she knew this. That was the moment it all changed. She seemed to know what Phoenix was thinking.

"You know, Phoenix, you can talk to me anytime."

That was it. That was what she'd been trying to ask for. With all her stutterings and chokings and butterflies, that was all she'd ever been trying to say. And there it was. A thing that was Said.

That was all she needed. Perhaps it was not a solution, not anywhere near what she would have loved to say to her. But it was what she had come for, and she had received it. And with it, a new state of mind, the *right* state of mind. Phoenix finally had that feeling of carefree bliss, and although she didn't know how long it would last, she was grateful for it. She suddenly felt filled with enthusiasm—she wasn't sure what for, but she knew she must find a way to use it, to grab life by the horns and take control for the first time in a long time, it would appear.

For two whole months, Phoenix was living in a waking dream. She would find Ms. Davis during lunch hours, or after classes—whenever she was free, and Phoenix was lonely. They would sit, and they would talk. Phoenix never understood the sheer power talking could hold. It was something she'd never done before. Her problems had always been her own, stirring at the back of her brain, remaining Said Not to all but her own mind.

Phoenix told her of her mother's death and her father's disappearance. Of the problems she'd had with the heating and electricity, and the struggle over the winter. Of her friendship with Juniper and how she'd found her that fateful day, and the trouble Juniper had experienced with Ash. Yes, Phoenix found herself telling everything, and she could not for the life of her figure out why. There was just something about this woman.

She learned a great deal about Phoenix in those eight weeks, but Phoenix learned a lot about her, too. Her name was Noelle. She had an older brother and a younger sister. And she had lived through pain. Phoenix couldn't say what that pain was—for it was not her story to tell. But what she could say was that now she understood the bewitching nature of her smile. Her smile was one that had struggled through tears; the type songwriters sing about. And her beauty shined brightest because of her seemingly infinite wisdom. She seemed to have all the answers, and advice that did more than just console, but actually healed. Yes, as Phoenix had mentioned, there was something about this woman, this peculiar angel called Noelle.

Ah yes, Phoenix was living in a waking dream—but dreams, as one well knows, can suddenly turn to nightmares.

CHAPTER 12

October 10ᵗʰ

It's strange thinking back over everything that's happened. It's very odd to me that a task such as writing a journal has brought back so much of my life, albeit things that I don't particularly like to dwell on very often. But then again, these things were my life—are my life—and they did happen. And they shaped the person I am today.

What I find most peculiar of all is everything that took place with Phoenix. I was happy—honored—when she came to talk to me. There was something about feeling that I was needed, that I could help, that I could make a positive difference to this girl's life. And that maybe, just maybe, I could have an influence that would mean that she didn't have to go through all the heartache—like the heartache I experienced—all on her own. That maybe I would be able to help her in a way that no-one was ever there to help me. Because she's still so young, and figuring out this world can be a horrendously difficult task. Especially when you're all on your own.

•••

It was sometime about a week before April that she came to her. Noelle had spent the morning sitting in a stuffy room for a staff meeting, and with the infinite lack of anything interesting to occupy her mind, she'd found it beginning to fill with snippets of days long past.

She watched their faces pour before her, heard their voices ringing in her ears, felt their touch upon her skin... One minute she was fine, and the next she was suffocating, the room around her suddenly too stifling for her to catch her breath. So, she stood up, excused herself from her colleagues, and swiftly exited the building. And that's how she found herself strolling down one of the paths that cut through the greenery of the school grounds.

"Ms. Davis?" Noelle turned to the young girl as she called her name, not even having realized her presence until she heard her voice. It took a moment for her to jumpstart her brain; to drag herself out of the dark mists that were swirling around inside her head, and into the real world.

Shaking herself free from the manacles of her mind, Noelle looked at the girl and smiled. "Miss Hudson."

"May I have a moment to speak with you?"

"Walk with me."

She joined Noelle on her stroll, and they continued to walk down the path that stretched out before them. For a while, they just walked in silence, and Noelle couldn't help but feel that whatever it was that this young student wanted to speak to her about, it wasn't related to either algebra or trigonometry. But she didn't mind, there was something about this particular student—Phoenix—that struck her as somewhat different from the rest. She never heard of any trouble with her work, she never saw her hanging around those who snuck out to smoke behind the bike sheds—in fact, she never really saw her hanging around many other students at all. Except for Juniper Chambers, that is…

And it was with that realization that it dawned on Noelle that she might have a pretty good idea what it was Phoenix might have wanted to say.

"So," she said, breaking the silence, "what did you want to speak with me about?"

Noelle watched as Phoenix's mouth opened, and then closed. A blush beginning to rise in her youthful cheeks as she averted her eyes. And once again Noelle felt a familiar pang in her chest, because somehow, as much as she lacked the ability to explain, she understood exactly how Phoenix felt. She didn't know how she understood, she just did. There was a nervousness there, a feeling from somewhere deep in one's soul that does nothing but question, question why one takes certain actions, question if one really needs this help one seeks, a question if one really deserves such help.

With her heart full of this strange sense of understanding, all Noelle could do was smile. "You know, Phoenix, you can talk to me anytime."

•••

In the next two months that were to follow my pathway encounter with Phoenix, I learned so much more about this girl than I think anyone else ever knew. This girl, this quiet girl, who seemed to have spent her life living in the shadows, had poured her soul out to me. And for the life of me, I couldn't understand why. I couldn't figure out what it was about me that made this girl feel so comfortable, so able and willing to tell these stories of her past, stories that crafted the person she had become. But what surprised me even more was how I found myself almost doing the same. There would be these things, little things, snippets of life that would show themselves in her history, and when they did, I found something in myself that latched on, that saw similarities, and as a result they bubbled to the surface.

And eventually, through the power of our conversations, I began to understand. There was something about her, something about the way she lived, and how she'd moved through space and time that reminded me so much of myself. Our memories were not the same, but god, they could have been. It is so hard to put into words how such a thing could be, but somehow everything made sense when we spoke. I never got the chance to be a mother, but sometimes I felt that maybe this was the closest thing.

But then there was something she told me—something about her father— something that put me in a position where I wish I had never been placed.

"He left one day last summer. I haven't seen him since."

Two sentences, eleven words, and suddenly I was stuck.

CHAPTER 13

"You know, to say that I'm alone would not be a statement that I could truly explain," Phoenix sat on her usual chair in the therapist's office, biting at her fingernails.

"And why is that, Phoenix?" The woman sat calmly on her seat, removing her glasses from her eyes to place them atop her head, and crossing her arms casually over her knees. "Do you feel alone?"

The young girl nodded. "Yes, I am alone, but perhaps not in the sense of the word. Yes, I lived alone for those months in a house with little but the ghosts of my past to keep me company, but people surrounded me every day—many, many people. However, even they did not see me. I don't think they ever had, and if so, then they simply choose to walk on by. But that never bothered me. It's the principle of the word, you see; the meaning behind it that says there is no-one there, no-one to help you, no-one to save you, no-one you can truly trust."

"Did you feel like you could trust Noelle?"

Phoenix nodded once again. "Yeah, for a while, at least."

The therapist sat forward in her chair and raised an eyebrow. "Only for a while? What happened after the while?"

"My world fell apart on a Friday," she replied blankly. "It was a day in mid-July; I remember the heat that filled the air on the morning that sparked the fire that I never saw coming. The fire that eventually burned me to the ground. I thought I had my person, but it would seem I did not. I never wanted to burden her with my ways, but I realized that I already had, and there was nothing I could change about what was Said. I keep thinking about those two months. Eight weeks. Fifty-six days. About everything I shared with her in that short time. That I was feeling lonely, and she was lovely, and she said we could work on that in the times to come. And I mistook that for a guarantee that there would be more times to come. But nothing is as simple as that."

"This is why you feel as if you landed in a place surrounded by complications?"

"Right," the young girl sighed. "We used to smile and say 'hi' every time we bumped into each other in the corridor, or on the stairs. It was like we had our own secret messaging service that meant every time we saw one another something would fly between us that stated, *I know you, and all these people around about us, they have no idea.* It was just us, trusting each other to hold the other's secrets safe from the world. Everything I had ever seen in my world of sleep had come into being. The caring nature of the mothering angel who'd told me that everything would be okay wasn't just a figment of my imagination anymore. She was here, she was with me, and I was comfortable with how life seemed. But then that all changed, and my perception of what Is and what Is Not was shaken once again."

"So, what changed?"

•••

Phoenix was sitting in the library when he came—running her eyes over the marvelous view of old books, observing the fingerprints that disturbed the dust, showing everyone the true color of the cover hidden beneath the coating of gray. She didn't even hear Mr. Cold come in but, when she turned, she found him standing right behind her.

"Miss Hudson, would you care to come with me?" He motioned toward the door, his hard features adding a chill to the summer air.

"Where?"

"To the principal's office."

"What for?"

The corner of his mouth twitched. "For a meeting. Don't fret, you're not in any trouble."

Hesitantly, she stood, and followed him out of the library to the principal's office. Mr. Cold wasn't the only thing that day to hold a chill. From the moment she entered the office, Phoenix felt the hair on the back of her neck stand up. A large table adorned the center of the room, and around it sat three people: the principal, a woman she didn't recognize, and Noelle.

•••

"I would love to recall the intricate details of what happened next," Phoenix exhaled, letting the silent tears run free once more.

"To explain all the seemingly insignificant things that somehow built up to a horrific ending. To make the world realize how I felt when I ran from the room, tears blurring my vision, the breath stuck in my chest. But I can't. In order to do that, I'd first have to understand it myself. And the more I try to wrap my head around it, the less sense I can make. So, I guess you must be presented with the short, sharp, yet far from sweet, version that sums up the blow I was given. The whole meeting was regarding my father—or, rather, the absence of my father. The time they spent explaining to me the reasons why it was their responsibility to notify social services was wasted, because by that point I was no longer listening. The only thing I could think about was Noelle. I'd put my trust in her, opened up to her, exposed the weakest points of my being, and I'd been betrayed."

"You felt like she'd betrayed your secrets?" asked the therapist, propping her hand against her chin. "That must have been very difficult for you."

Phoenix almost laughed through her tears. "All I could hear after that was the ringing in my ears as if a bomb had just been dropped mere inches from my head. I remember that my face and neck were wet with tears. Long black lines of mascara streaked my skin. My breath shook as it escaped from my heaving chest. My vision only a collage of blurred colors, bleeding into one. I couldn't feel. I couldn't speak. I couldn't think. Only one thing played in my head, over and over again, stuck on repeat. One word. One syllable. *Why?"* She choked on her tears.

The therapist leaned over and handed her a box of tissues.

"She told me that it was nothing personal, that she was just doing her job," Phoenix sniffed, "but I found that after that, I couldn't even look at her. I couldn't look at her. Because if I did, all I saw was every conversation we ever had, the concern in those deep blue eyes, and the frown when she wasn't convinced by whatever I had left Said Not—because she could sense those things about me. The smile that made her cheeks so plump, and caused little lines to appear beside the corner of her eyes... I couldn't do that. I couldn't bear to remember all that, because it didn't exist anymore. And I couldn't stand it. I couldn't stand to look at her, because it was a reminder of everything I'd lost. Every story I'd told her about the scars in my brain where people used to be: my mother, my father, my best friend. Everything I'd never—and *will* never— have back. And that hurt me more than anything. Knowing that it was all gone. That I was alone again and facing whatever social services would bring down on me. It didn't seem fair that my entire life had to change, and Noelle got to continue on as if nothing ever happened."

"And do you believe that?" the therapist enquired, "that Noelle got to continue as if nothing ever happened?"

Phoenix shrugged. "I don't know. But it just didn't seem worth the pain."

"So, how did you deal with that?"

"I avoided her. Whenever I was supposed to have a class with her, I wouldn't show up. Whenever I saw her from along a corridor, I would turn around and leave. Whenever she happened to be standing in a room that I was headed for, I would run away before she had to chance to notice my presence." Phoenix wiped her eyes with the saturated tissue in her hand.

"And she never came looking for me. She never sought me out to explain why she did what she did. She never questioned why I refused to attend her classes. She never apologized for the Noelle-shaped hole she left in my heart. It's so difficult to mourn something when you're both still standing there. Going through daily life. Refusing to look at each other. Pretending that everything is normal. But none of this was normal."

•••

Phoenix was taken into foster care a week after the conversation in the principal's office. The night before the social worker came for her was one she didn't think she'd ever forget. She'd arrived home as she did every evening—to the chilled emptiness of the small cottage, the cooler atmosphere coming as a relief for once against the heat of the late summer sun outwith. For a moment she'd just stared... at everything; her eyes drinking in every minute detail of the place she'd called home for the past fifteen years.

From the edges of the worn sofa, her eyes wandered to the grand bookshelf that stood so proudly in the corner of the room. The books within looking so peaceful where they perched, completely unaware of the fate that was staring them in the face once this home became nothing more than an uninhabited cottage on the outskirts of town. But perhaps the books had their own problems to deal with; the hundreds and thousands of unread words just bursting with the knowledge of wars long lost, and cities both fanciful and forgotten.

Phoenix sighed, tearing her eyes away from the mahogany structure, picking up her violin from beside the couch, and padding slowly through the desolate hallway.

Creeping into her mother's room—for what she feared to be the last time—she closed the door firmly to the rest of the world and sat lightly at the end of her mom's bed. Closing her eyes, she let the floral scents enter her body and entwine themselves throughout her brain. She positioned her violin under her chin, and began to play, as she had done so many times before, ignoring the salty tears that were now rolling slowly down her cheeks.

Soon, the euphonic tunes were completely entangled with the rosy aromas that floated so delicately around her. It's just as they say— how strange it is that a melody can sound so much like a memory. And as she sat playing with her eyes closed, she expected to see her mom standing before her. She expected to see her smiling at her as she played, the smell of the room and of her being merging as one whilst she played for her.

But it wasn't her mother that Phoenix saw before her; it was Noelle. She stopped abruptly, her violin giving a small shriek as the jerking of her hand pulled the strings in a whimsical nature. Her eyes flew open. Only the emptiness of the room looked back at her. She was almost surprised, though she didn't know why. A second ago her immediate surroundings had been filled with a strange warmth, and now, there was nothing but the dust flowing from the old curtains to keep her company.

•••

"That was such a strange night," sighed Phoenix, her tears beginning to dry into hard lines on her face.

"How so?"

"When I was playing the violin… Why had I been thinking of Noelle? It was her fault everything had to change. It was her doing that had me sitting in the sanctum of sweet saturninity that had once been my mom's bedroom for the last time.

"And it made me feel guilty. Like I'd betrayed my parents, as if I'd tried to replace them with this idealized figure of imperfection. It was all my fault, after all, right? I was the one who let my father down. I should have supported him, helped him more, been strong enough for the both of us. I was the one who failed Juniper. I was her best friend, her only true confidant, and I'd let that boy get away with how he treated her. I'd let her stew in her own mind, let the fear and the loneliness bubble away to such an extent that it spilled over. I should have been there to comfort her, to let her know that she was worth so much more than either Ash or her parents ever let her believe. I should have told her that she wasn't alone."

"Oh, Phoenix," the therapist said slowly, shaking her head slightly in that show of sympathy she sometimes gave, "I'm sorry you feel that way, but please tell me that you know it isn't true?"

"Well, then the realization hit me," Phoenix exhaled, almost smiling through her tears. "There was a reason for it all. For the way I felt. It all linked back to that which is Said Not, because of the fear it is Acceptable Not. I realized that in all that time I spent blaming Noelle for what she did, I never stopped dreaming about her, I never had a day where she left my mind. Because despite everything, it didn't change what she had done for me. It didn't change how she had helped me. It didn't mean she hadn't saved me.

"It wasn't all my fault; she'd helped me see that. My father was sick, he'd been sick for a long time, and it wasn't my fault that he never sought help. He was an adult, who'd been dealing with his own mind for longer than I had even been alive. I was only his child; there was nothing I could have done.

"Juniper had been sick too, with a similar type of sickness. I had done my best to be there for her, to offer her support. I'd been her nearest and dearest friend for all those years, and that was what was needed of me. I should not feel guilty that things ended the way they did. It was not my responsibility to save them. I cannot blame myself."

The therapist let loose a sigh that sounded almost of relief. "Well, I'm glad to hear that. I think that's a very important realization for you to have, and a much healthier way of looking at things."

"And do you know how I came to that realization?"

"How?"

"Because of her: Noelle—the person who could, and maybe forever will, break my heart over and over again without ever being present. The one who changed it all. And I can't risk the chance that I might never see her again." The young girl almost laughed as she spoke, her words coming now from a stream straight from her brain, not stopping to be dwelled upon before coming out of her mouth. And at that moment it was as if she finally understood the point of therapy, could finally make sense out of all these things that had happened, as if she suddenly had some sort of answer. "I know what I have to do. I have to make it Said. I have to bring it into the world of what Is. But first, I have to make that world."

•••

So, there she stood. And mentally, where that was, exactly, was something Phoenix didn't know. But every moment of every day, she thought of her, and it hurt; it physically hurt. Not her smile, or sparkling eyes, not her strong personality, or caring nature, those were not the things that caused Phoenix's pain.

But to know that she would never have that if she were never to speak to Noelle again. To know that her smile would no longer be for Phoenix, her strength would no longer support her, and the care would be withheld.

How could Phoenix possibly try to explain to her what she had felt? How the simple things that she brought meant so much to her? And the things she had seen in her dreams? And how all of that somehow won over the feelings of betrayal? Because she knew now that what she did, she only did to try and help her.

She had gone over the words so many times in her head. And if Noelle could hear her at those moments, hear all the whizzing thoughts that were pinging back and forth inside her brain, then she would know everything Phoenix was never able to tell her before. She would tell her everything: about the day she first noticed her in the classroom, and the day Noelle first noticed her back; about the dreams and how they made her feel that someone was there with her, even before they'd ever spoken; and about how she had become her muse.

Phoenix would tell her why she reacted the way she did about the meeting and how they were dealing with her father's departure. She would make her see why she was hurt, help her to understand instead of just shutting her out.

Then… well, then Phoenix would apologize. She would say how sorry she was for everything, the sort of everything she didn't even know about yet. Explain that she didn't mean for her to become the fixation she had. Phoenix would tell her she was sorry for wanting that which was Acceptable Not. She would tell her she was sorry for dreaming about her, about wanting her to be more than she could possibly be. She would tell her she was sorry for loving her the way she did.

As previously stated, Phoenix did not mean to fall, and certainly not so hard, but once she had, she couldn't get back up. And she didn't think she wanted to.

So, what did she feel? She didn't know. A mixture of so many emotions was swirling nauseatingly around inside her head, and the undeniable sense of nerves that she could not shift was most certainly not helping the situation. Did she have doubts about what she was going to do? Yes, there were many. It made her unsure; she didn't know what to do. A great tightness clasped around her lungs, her eyes not sure whether to smile or cry, her heart not knowing if it should sing or die.

How she got there, she didn't know, but she would find her way out, she would find a way to answer this question. She would find her voice, she would make a decision, and she would stick by it, for what would come to be the rest of her life.

Phoenix saw Noelle up ahead, walking toward her. It was not surprising this time. She had asked to meet her here. She had said that she needed to talk to her. So, there she stood still, feeling the nauseating butterflies deep in her gut. Light tingling broke out across her body, and a sweat began to build on her top lip. Her mouth felt like cotton wool, and she had to swallow a few times just to feel comfortable enough to speak.

And then there she was, smiling sympathetically at Phoenix, as she always did, those little lines appearing at the corner of her eyes.

"Phoenix," she said, "I'm sorry about…"

"No," Phoenix cut in. She didn't know why she did that. She was apologizing. Phoenix didn't think she wanted her to apologize anymore. It wasn't in her plan. Phoenix coughed awkwardly, hoping to get out all she wanted to say before she lost it. "I have something to explain to you."

And there it came, all the words pouring out of her mouth like a floodgate had been opened.

"You were my inspiration, my hero, the person I looked up to the most. You were the only person there for me at the time when I was most alone. You listened, and you cared, and you helped me through it. And then you sat there, in that room, with the principal, and that, that… *woman*, and you watched me cry so hard that I hyperventilated. You walked away and left me gasping. And since then, I've been stuck with you in my head and my heart, and nothing I can do will make me stop thinking about you."

Phoenix paused for breath, refusing to look up at her face, terrified to see her reaction.

"And the worst part?" Phoenix felt the tears start to swell in her eyes. "Is that I…" She choked, feeling the cotton come back, hot tears beginning to spill slowly down her cheeks. Deep breaths. Start again. Just say it. Make is Said, at least. "I love you. I have done for quite some time now. I love you like a mother; I wish you were my mother. And for that, *I'm* sorry."

Then came the moments Phoenix had been dreading. She stood still, rubbing her sweaty palms together, hoping against hope that she didn't just laugh and walk away. She lifted her tear-filled eyes to look upon Noelle's face. She was just standing there. Staring back at her. Her brow furrowed into that concerned frown Phoenix liked so much. She could feel her heart palpitating in her chest. Her breath being taken away as it skipped beats. And then, Noelle opened her mouth. God, Phoenix had never felt so light-headed before.

"Okay."

That was it? The relief washed over her faster than she expected. Her limbs felt as if they may just fall off with the sudden release of tension. It may not be a perfect answer, but she didn't leave, she didn't laugh, she didn't stop to tell her how wrong that was. She just said, *okay*.

Phoenix cleared my throat once more. "Okay?"

Noelle nodded. Her brow still furrowed. "Okay. That wasn't what I was expecting—in fact, that was probably the last thing I was expecting—but okay. We'll have to talk about this, of course. But not right now. Tomorrow, maybe. But not today. Today, I need to stop. Think. And tomorrow, tomorrow, we will talk about this."

Placing a hand on her shoulder, Noelle squeezed it lightly, and Phoenix found it strangely comforting. She had forgotten what it was like to receive a reassuring touch from the adults who seem to care for you; she hadn't seen a parent figure in so long.

And Noelle, well, Phoenix could probably get away with letting slip one of her secrets. Noelle and Phoenix held one major thing in common, and that was the yearning for something that is missing. For Phoenix, a parent; for Noelle, a child. Phoenix always thought it was that knowledge that really gave her the courage to do this. If humans were jigsaw pieces, then they would fit perfectly.

She turned to leave, and Phoenix let loose a sigh of relief. "Thank you, Noelle, thank you so much."

Noelle stopped and turned her head back toward Phoenix. She smiled and gave a quick wink, before turning back around, and disappearing out of sight once more.

A bird flew free ahead of Phoenix's gaze, and she smiled. That was what she would do; she would soar like a bird, and be able to fly wherever she pleased, whenever it suited her. She could not help the smile that grew across her face, as her eyes closed, and she imagined the happiness that she could soon have. As she opened her eyes once more, she let loose a small yelp of glee at her prospective outcome.

Phoenix knew she would still be facing the possibility of the next few years in foster care if they couldn't track down her father. She knew that it was very possible that she'd never again be able to see her little cottage and step back into the life she'd come to know. But she also knew that now, at least she might not be doing it alone.

Why was she so happy about this, one may wonder? Well, it wasn't perfect, but nothing is. Especially when it comes to love. Because love is all about the timings, the Then and the Now; the truth, of what is Said and what is Said Not; the circumstance, of what is Acceptable and what is Acceptable Not. But, most of all love is, well, quite simply… *complicated.*

Printed in Great Britain
by Amazon

63359252R00092